"This was surely Great Dog himself."

The Ugly Dachshund

G. B. Stern

Illustrations by K. F. Barker

J. N. TOWNSEND PUBLISHING
EXETER, NEW HAMPSHIRE
1998

Printed in Canada

Published by
J. N. Townsend Publishing
12 Greenleaf Drive
Exeter, New Hampshire 03833
1-800-333-9883
603-778-9883
Fax: 603-772-1980

ISBN: 1-880158-15-9

For Gerald

FOREWORD

The kind of book that people refer to as a "gem" has a way of slipping out of sight, like a very small diamond loosed from its ring-setting and vanishing in the tall grass. This happens often in times of turmoil, as during a world war, when people turn their minds to darker, weightier matters and only much later, with peace restored, wonder whatever happened to the small things that sparkled.

The Ugly Dachshund, by G.B. Stern, a noted Jane Austen scholar, was one of those. A few people of a certain age remember it wistfully, the tale of the Great Dane raised among dachshunds, and search futilely for the copy they're sure they had, back in the 1930s or '40s. It's gone, of course. Gems vanish.

Against all odds, Tono the melancholy Dane has been restored to us.

His world is the sunny world of the carefree and well-to-do in Provence between the Wars, where we meet Tono; the dachshund family; the worldly visiting griffon Voltaire; and a nasty piece of work from Hollywood, Dulcibel the Pomeranian. Jane Austen herself might have assembled the cast and woven their concerns, their loves, jealousies, religion, and snobberies and their complex relations with the humans, called "Legs."

World War II is still only a smudge on the horizon, reported by the well-traveled Voltaire, who tells the dachshunds of a new, steely Germany quite different from the elves-and-cobblers country of their family fairy tales, In Provence, though, Tono has more immediate problems.

For those who enjoy a good moral, it's possible, I suppose, to read *The Ugly Dachshund* as a fable. Tono, assuming himself a dachshund, grieves bitterly that the Legs feed him raw meat instead of the cooked delicacies the others enjoy, and never pick him up or cuddle him or call him sweet. Like Anderson's duckling, he feels himself an outcast, a pariah, too inept even to squeeze through the fence like the others. His only consolation is an occasional mystic vision of the almighty Great Dog, who appears to him sometimes in polished parquet or ponds and, once, in a mirror.

It's possible to consider this a fable about the troubles we make for ourselves when we misunderstand our true natures.

That said, we can relax and lean through its window onto the world of dog in all its variousness, including Eva, the swaggering, seafaring dachshund who sings sailors' chanteys and quotes John Masefield. This is a gentle novel, a respectful novel, a dignified novel, but — like one of Jane Austen's own— it is also very, very funny.

Let us rejoice that a lost gem has been found and rescued from the tall grass of oblivion.

Barbara Holland

"'They are very pretty children indeed, all of them, with the exception of one only, and he has certainly not succeeded.'"

"...But what did he now see in the clear water? He saw his own reflection; but it was no longer the ugly, dirty, green-grey bird—no, it was a proud, princely swan!"

Hans Andersen, *The Ugly Duckling*

The Ugly Dachshund

CHAPTER ONE

"I KNOW THAT the other dachshunds don't feel like this," Tono admitted. "I can't help it: when the Legs expect visitors, I *have* to be standing on the front steps. It's a mysterious compulsion."

Elsa looked down her nose, which was a very long way, and wished her companion would not use words of which he did not understand half the meaning. If he enjoyed being one of a formal welcoming group with the Supreme Legs and the Master Legs, why, let him; that was his own affair.

But it was no more and no less than just something he wanted to do.

"I suppose," she mused, the March sun stroking her smooth tan-coloured back to a hotter ginger, "I suppose if you were a Dalmatian and wanted to run under a dog-cart, you'd call that a mysterious compulsion as well, wouldn't you?"

"I don't know," replied Tono cautiously, puzzled by this sudden intrusion, from nowhere, of a dogcart, "What's a Dalmatian? Is it a Wunman-dog, like Erda?" - for he had heard the Legs say: "She's a one-man dog," of Elsa's elder daughter, that beautiful black pochette filled with love for the Supreme

Legs only, as a roly-poly pudding is dark and soft with jam. And he thought this an opportunity to pump Elsa, older and wiser than himself, as to whether he too had a chance to qualify as a Wunman-dog.

Elsa moved her front paws impatiently, but could not be bothered to reply. Tono was really not very bright ("May Dog forgive the under-statement!"), and this sudden burst of spring weather, so bold as to be almost unseemly, after three weeks of drenching Provençal rains, was making her too dreamy to

"What's a Dalmatian?"

3

keep on enlightening him about this and that. "Dreamy," with Elsa, was a synonym for wishing food would come to her, instead of steadily, persistently, going to food. They were lying on the little patch of grass outside the door which led to the kitchen and pantry premises, and Elsa thought she could detect, in the bustling movements of the Apron Legs within, a thrilling promise of noonday dinner on its way.

Elsa loved the noon. There was all the difference, she would argue in her materialistic German fashion, between noon and moon. The one was a substantial dish of biscuit and meat and vegetables and gravy and rice, all cooked up together; whereas the other, unsubstantial and clammy, floated a little way above the eucalyptus trees, and always rather irritated Elsa, who had an unromantic nature, and had already had three families (the Legs in their coarse way called them "litters," but it was not considered etiquette among the dogs even to recognise a word like that) without ever having been in love.

Tono rose and stretched himself. "Well I'd better go along. The car will be here at any moment now, and it would look so bad if I weren't waiting."

Elsa was shocked: "You can't go now. It's dinnertime. Who is this visitor, anyhow, that you're making so much fuss about?"

"It's a Relative Legs. I think she's out of the same basket as the Supreme Legs. His elder sister. She's going to stay for some time. You ought to come into the dining-room more; then you'd hear what was going on."

But Elsa preferred the kitchen premises, where plenty went on, and plenty dropped beneath the table; where the air was always warm and savoury, and where the Staff Legs were not perpetually expecting bursts of sentimental devotion or touching instances of fidelity. Let Tono squander his heart on the Master Legs; let her pretty brunette daughter, Erda, follow the Supreme Legs wherever he went, pattering at his feet, her broad delicious paws turned anxiously outwards —"Thank Dog, Erda has crooked legs. Much more useful than brains, when you have the bad luck to be born a bitch" —but she, Elsa, was a philosopher, aware that for creatures living low and close to the ground, not reared high up and away from all matters of true importance, only four things counted, one for each foot: food, food, sex and food.

"Lie down," she now bade Tono, "and stop fidgeting. The car has only just gone to the station. You've plenty of time to eat your dinner first, and then to go and say your piece from the steps."

Tono wished that Elsa, on the rare occasions when she hobnobbed with the rest of them, would not be quite so peremptory and experienced. She might even be the mother of the other dachshunds, Erda and Eva, and the twins, Fafnir and Wotan, but she was not *his* mother. Sometimes, indeed, he suspected he was an orphan, and then he would heave a conventional sigh or two and murmur gravely: "Terrible thing to be an orphan, terrible!" without, however, being able to see that Elsa was much of a spiritual sanctuary to the exuberant twins, who at this very moment were proving to their own dissatisfaction that, while the law of gravity assisted them from the top of the long flight of steps downwards from terrace to terrace, it had no such power to attract them from the bottom up again. The stairs were far too steep for those little squirming tan-coloured sausages, so they yelped and squealed and rolled about, and gave an impression of a garden dripping with dachshunds.

Eva and the twins were relics of Elsa's last whelping; nobody quite knew, not even Elsa herself, what constituted their twinship. Erda the Beautiful was the only one left from the family-before-last. Elsa, a casual mother, would say when reproached with her coolness: "I make no differences. I love all my puppies alike." But far back in the first family of eight had been Sieglinde, her gold-headed girl. Sieglinde had not died young; she had simply been given away by the Legs. Elsa always held it against them. They had failed to grasp that in the obstinate little web of instincts and unreason which is a dachshund's mind and soul and memory all closely knitted together, Sieglinde counted as the kingdom, and the other seven as nothing at all. Even now, when she mentioned Sieglinde, her bark softened and her chilly black nose grew warm.

The White Linen Legs came out with Elsa's dish of smoking desire. Elsa hurled herself upon it almost before he had laid it on the ground; hardly pausing to gabble, from old conventional habit, her maternal-minded grace: "I only eat to keep up my strength," which she had learned was an expedient argument while carrying her first load of puppies.

Erda, Eva and the twins, attracted by the smell, came leaping and tumbling along from outlying portions of the garden and villa. Erda was already more than a year old, and was allotted her own dish; but Eva and the twins had to share, and loud were the cries: "She pushed me!" for Eva appeared to think that to drown her brothers in the soup need not be an act for which she would afterwards deserve punishment; she deemed them so puppyish for their age, the twins; so backward in their response to the promise of life and adventure; they just shoved each other about and flumped down the steps, and grunted and squeaked and lost their way; while already Eva had made an intrepid adventure of all the garden paths; already, a small black glossy mountaineer, she had clambered, defying the laws of gravity, to the swimming-pool under the oleanders at the summit of the terraces; and, standing on the marble seat which ran round three sides of it, looked long-ingly past the tops of the pine and eucalyptus trees, to something deep blue and shimmering, far down and far away, which the Legs called "the sea." Except an American journalist Legs who had called it "the ocean," and a Classical Legs who had called it "Thalassa."

Eva was an Elizabethan in spirit. The sea called to her, the distance beckoned her, waves murmured an enchanted song in her floppy silken ears.

"All I ask," she confided in Erda, using the first words that came into her head, though they sounded perhaps a little grandiose, "all I ask is a tall ship and a star to steer her by. That's all I ask." And then she stamped her paw and yapped impatiently: "Oh, why wasn't I born a *dog!*" And Erda, frightened, scampered off to tell an un-sympathetic Elsa; who, twisting round to bur-row her nose hard into her flanks, wrinkling it fiercely in the quest for some invisible annoy-ance, remarked that all Eva really asked was a condition powder, and she hoped the Legs would give it to her quick.

Meanwhile, on this day of the arrival of

the Relative Legs, Tono's dinner bore witness to Tono's daily tragedy. For, while the other dachshunds had their food nicely cooked and mashed, with a lot of trouble taken, Tono's consisted of about two pounds of raw meat flung at him without any preparation; no garnishing of parsley, nor Sauce Hollandaise, nor that neat surround of aspic symmetrically decorated with anchovy and olive; nothing to tempt the coy appetite; just an atmosphere of: *"Mon Dieu,* we cannot be bothered to cook Tono's dinner. *Quelle ideé!* Let him make the best of it raw."

And that was just an example, one in a thousand, of that queer dislocation which separated his daily life from the other dachshunds. It showed itself in ways so slight that perhaps a less sensitive dog might not have noticed. The Supreme Legs and the Master Legs never picked him up by the scruff and landed him on their knees, as they frequently did to the others; nor tucked him cosily under their arm. They did not fondle and pet him, using small foolish endearments, but hit him in a hearty fashion, with phrases of robust affection. And oh, they never, never called him "sweet." Often, when he gambolled with the others, the Legs laughed loud and in mockery; when, under the table, he flumped down on a Visitor Legs' foot, he heard groans and felt himself shoved away. Why? They did not push the others away. And why, again, when the others squeezed their yards of boneless body through the wooden slats of the fence separating the villa grounds from the road where they were forbidden to go, why, hurling himself after, did he always get bruised and hurt, but remain ignominiously on this side of the slats?

He came to the sad conclusion that he was not only an orphan but a pariah; pariah rhyming as a matter of course with Maria; yet he did not wish the other dachshunds to dub him a dog-with-a-grievance; so he never mentioned his pariah obsession, and Elsa had no chance to turn up her melancholy nose at his pronunciation.

Tono's natural disposition was cheerful. But, after adjuring himself sternly for a long time not to go imagining things," he had to give in to evidence that somehow he could not quite get into alignment with the other dachshunds. He yearned for the Master Legs, especially, to pick him up and carry him in the crook of his arm . . . in the crook of his arm . . . Tono trembled with ecstasy at the mere idea. Yet it had never happened; at least, not that he could clearly remember. Somewhere far back in a confused recollection of different surroundings and fuzzy shapes tumbling in a basket—or was it a prenatal dream?—the Master Legs had come along and said, divinely discriminating: *"I'll have this one!"*

CHAPTER TWO

YET ALWAYS in the background was the Vision and the consolation.

The first time Dog had appeared to him—

No, there had been no tangible first time; gradually Tono had become aware of glimpses every now and then, among the polished parquet and gleaming walnut furniture of the villa; glimpses so stupendous and yet so fleeting that he was hardly aware of them except as a dim sense of comfort, of not being quite alone. And once, when he was looking into the pool, crossed and dappled by a flicker of oleander blossoms and silver twigs of eucalyptus and a tangle of hurrying shadow-clouds, he thought he saw what he dared not as yet give a name, even to himself.

He always linked his first clear vision of Great Dog with his first passionate awakening to injustice. Until that day, he had pretended that he was a silly little Tono who imagined things, and of course the Legs' treatment of him was scrupulously equal to their treatment of the other dachshunds: Elsa and Erda, and their lively brethren, now forgotten, who had been in the same basketful as Erda.

Tono could not bear to dwell in a world where the Legs were not fair and just and kind, caring for all their little animals alike, merciful to them all alike, and, if need be, punishing them all alike. So he went on denying any less oriented existence.

Until a certain memorable day when a visitor, a Legs-of-no-Importance, was expected from Venice. Tono politely welcomed him from the steps, as usual; two steps below the Supreme Legs, three steps above the Butler Legs. The Master Legs was driving the car, and he called out, as they stopped:

"He's brought Neddie. And a present. A mirror. A real beauty. Early Venetian." And two objects were lifted from the car: a chubby brown Legs, small and active, and a large wooden packing-case. Both were courteously rejoiced over by the Supreme Legs, though Tono fancied a shade more rejoicing over the packing-case; and one or the other, he didn't know which, was declared to be just what was wanted for the north wall of the inner court-yard, and must go up at once. One was apparently eight years old; the other rather more: "At a rough guess," said the Legs-of-no-Impor-tance, "late sixteenth century."

The scene shifted to the long terrace beyond the sitting-room, and the Chubby Legs rather fearfully throwing a ball, Tono and Elsa and Erda scampering after it as fast as their short crooked little legs could carry them; only Tono always outpaced the others and was the first to come thundering back (it sounded like thunder in his own ears, because a chase after any flying object was so exciting). And when it was picked up and held aloft again, he and the other dachshunds bounded all around the Chubby Legs, with cascades of barking. Why the Chubby Legs should have suddenly fallen down flat on his back and howled, Tono never understood ("I *might* have *just* touched him with the tips of my paws . . ."), but he was willing to take his share of the blame with the others, when the Master Legs and the Legs-of-No-Importance came running to the rescue, and heard the sobbed-out story of damage and woe. But Erda and Elsa got off scot-free; the whole blame went to Tono; Tono was shut up in the garage for the rest of the day, a violation of justice too glaring for him to pretend any more that mere imagination was playing him tricks.

That evening, after the Chubby Legs had been put to bed, he was released and forgiven, and acquiesced humbly in the forgiveness; and wandered restlessly round the villa, sighing every now and then; thinking it might be a good thing, perhaps, to retire into a monastery, and fast, and die of fasting, and see if the Legs would realise then that he was no worse than the other little dachshunds; in fact, rather better in lots of quiet unobtrusive ways. In this mood, he strayed into a ground-floor spare-room not often used, and through its further door on to forbidden ground.

The inner courtyard was a pause in the very heart of the villa; a square cloistered space, Moorish style, with the sky resting on it lightly like a lid, archways of slender white pillars, a small square of green grass which always looked as though it had just been enamelled, and a stone fountain in the middle. But against the walls it was furnished like a room, some quiet meditative room in an ancient Catholic country: Spain or old Germany.

The courtyard was usually dark at this time of evening; but tonight the light had been left brightly burning in the dining-room beyond, and the Butler Legs was clearing the table after dinner. Tono did not care to take his hurt feelings indoors to the sitting-room, where doubtless Erda lay cuddled on the couch with her nose thrust cosily against the Supreme Legs' thigh, and one of her ears turned inside-out to show its lining of bright tan plush; nor into the kitchen where, doubtless again, Elsa in her businesslike way was seeing what could be done about the remains which had been carried out from the dinnertable. He went moping and mooching round and round the cloistered court, finding in it some not unsoothing resemblance to the monastery whither he intended to take his broken heart and bury it like a bone.

Suddenly, through a hole in the wall framed in dusky gold, a hole which Tono was convinced had never been there before, he saw his Vision.

He saw Dog.

Not blurred and wavering this time, not dimly discernible through shadow crossed by eucalyptus twigs, but clearly and boldly, standing quite still, steadily regarding him with an air of noble dignity, of power held in leash for kindness' sake; standing ten times larger than any mortal dog of Tono's ken; his glossy coat brindled between black and tawny orange, his ears set high and carried proudly erect; his arched neck, his muscular shoulders, his legs long and straight and splendid, his dogly tail, his broad muzzle, his eyes yellow and benign—

Yes, this was surely Great Dog himself, impossibly huge and improbably beautiful, revealed in one dramatic flash to comfort and reassure his sorrowful little disciple.

And, while Tono gazed and gazed, the light which flooded the courtyard from the dining-room was switched off, and velvety blackness blotted out the Vision.

Tono's was a nature curved for pure adoration, as a stoup is curved to hold holy water; and this experience filled his days and nights with a mellow afterglow which did not wholly fade, although he had been unable to obtain access to the inner courtyard again. Perhaps this was an unacknowledged relief. Awe was an emotion too massive to cramp into his trotting, busy, daily round of dwarf pleasures and dwarf pains, little running currents of delicate smell and sagacious warning, tiny savours beyond his reach, pigmy disappointments, and desires which, though not ignoble, had their dwelling-place close to the ground. Still perplexed by that slight lack of coordination in his viewpoint when compared with that of the other dachshunds, that perpetual odd Illusion of matter and motivation slipped a bit awry, Tono was now able to accept life on these terms without whine or snuffle, for he had been privileged above other dachshunds. He had seen Dog.

At rare intervals, as he dashed about through the rooms of the villa, or barked at Eva dancing on her toes and checking him from the opposite shore of the swimming-pool, he would imagine that Dog was just about to appear before him; but each time, provokingly, the Legs would choose just that instant to call him away from wherever he was. Still, even these elusive glimpses were like whispers that the original Vision had been more solid than a dream.

Dreams, what were dreams? Elsa or Erda giving little sharp movements, twitches on the floor, little cries in their sleep. "Dreaming?" the Master Legs would say in his charming voice. Perhaps he said it also of Tono, while the latter lay curled asleep on the rug in front of the fire, or stretched out-of-doors on the hot stone or in the compassionate shade. He wished that, dreaming, he could yet at the same time be awake and hear him say it: "Dreaming? Poor little chap!" so kindly and so tenderly. But wher-

ever you went, scuttling down those dark archways, good dreams and dragon dreams, Dog was
not there.

CHAPTER THREE

THE RELATIVE LEGS had brought her own little dog, this time, for a long stay at the villa. She was carrying him under her arm in a determined fashion as she alighted from the car, and greeted first the Butler Legs, then the Master Legs, and then, to show she was not in the least intimidated by an elder brother, the Supreme Legs.

"I've brought Voltaire," she announced, not without a touch of defiance.

The Supreme Legs looked at Voltaire with distaste: "A grigon. How detestable!"

"He comes of a long race of champions," retorted the Relative Legs, spirited and white-haired. "And he's quivering with intelligence, which is more than one can say for *some* people's dogs." Without any apparent relevance, she turned to Tono and gave him an affectionate shove in the flank: "And how is our Tono-bungay? our Wee Willie Winkie? our Tiny Tim?" They were in the sitting-room by now, and Tono immediately tried to clamber into her lap, supposing, not unnaturally, that her greetings were an invitation.

"*That's* the way!" the Relative Legs encouraged him falsely with her voice, while actually holding him off with both hands and feet. "Just a leaf fluttering to the ground; a bubble; a creature of ethereal lightness and grace—"

"You know," interposed the Master Legs, laughing, but his tone showing clearly that he wished the Relative Legs had remained at home in Paris, "you're embarrassing Tono. He takes compliments at their surface value."

Tono, standing patiently beside the Relative Legs, with his head slightly turned away from her, shifted his weight and sighed. To be noticed with politeness and affection was all very well, but he had always heard that "praise to the muzzle is open Schlamozzel." And besides, he did not wish Voltaire to overhear his full name, Tono-bungay, which he thought sounded affected and literary and silly, and which he never used, even on his big leather collar with brass studs; he could not decide whether to be pleased that they distinguished him from the other dachshunds by this more important collar, or to grieve that they did not dress all their little animals the same.

Voltaire apparently had not heard; he was making a running tour of inspection over the pattern of the carpet at the window end of the room where the light was best. His back and tail looked highly knowledgeable:

"*C'est Bokhara? Mais non*; like so many other experts I make the mistake and confuse a carpet of the Tekke tribe with Bokhara. This is a Tekke Turcoman of the nineteenth century and a very finely woven specimen. The owner of this villa I perceive to be a Legs of taste and discrimination."

The Supreme Legs remarked: "I think your dog wants to be put out," thus measuring out payment for a few old scores of childhood.

His sister replied crisply: "You don't understand Voltaire; he's not a silly puppy; he's a mature, sensitive, highly educated type."

"I regret if I've hurt his feelings by my suggestion that he has mortal parts like the rest of us."

"Oh, you haven't. Voltaire's a cynic."

"No doubt that rôle suits him better than had he chosen to be a gigolo."

"Originally I called him Chummy, but then I altered it. He's not chummy; he's not even a oneman dog. He notices everything and cares for nobody. I've named my favourite armchair: 'Qui Vive.' Why?"—though nobody had asked why. "Because he's always on it."

"That hardly even begins to be funny," said the Master Legs cheerfully.

"Yes, it does."

"Does what?"

"Begin to be funny."

"No, it doesn't."

Tono had been listening attentively, turning his head from one to the other; as usual, humbly desirous of picking up some potent information from the Legs which might be of use to him in after-life; anxious that not one pearl should be dropped unheeded from the thread of wisdom on which they were all-too-loosely strung. But for once it really did seem as though the pearls were too deep for the diver. Or, in other words, that none of it made sense.

Except that bit about Voltaire *not* being a Wunman-dog.

He felt a growing desire to know the stranger better; and was glad when he was given to understand from the Legs that he might take Voltaire out-of-doors, show him round and introduce him to the others.

The last remark which Tono overheard, as he and the griffon trotted through the open French windows, was from the Relative Legs enquiring brightly: "And what's this I hear about your having bought a yacht?"

Tono wanted to make the best impression on Voltaire; so he led him first along the paved path under the double row of orange trees rich with golden fruit. "This is almost our nicest place, just for a short stroll," he remarked chattily; "especially with so much rain as we've been having lately. Though I suppose you think, like all dogs who live in big Northern cities, that it's always sunshine in this part of the world. But I assure you"—using the weather as a topic for as long as it would serve—"it's sometimes very muddy here in the early spring, and then the other dachshunds prefer this path because their bellies don't get wet; somehow that never seems to bother me so much; I suppose I manage mine better. What is it?"

For Voltaire had stopped dead in his walk, to stare at Tono attentively. His round popping eyes bulged; at any moment they might burst. . . .

"Would you care to see our collection of cactuses?" Tono enquired, a little uncomfortable under such scrutiny.

The griffon dragged his glance away from some trance of incredulous joy, and signified his willingness to inspect cactuses: "a plant most formidably intelligent."

So they trotted on again, well matched and loquacious, up to the next terrace, and back along the path and up again, in a series of zig-zags. Every now and then, Voltaire was compelled to give his companion a curious sidelong glance, as though gradually becoming aware of an exhalation almost too divinely funny to be true.

"Here they are!" With a showman's pride, Tono waved his paw towards a garden of fantastic monstrosities, sprouting in stiff and hairy growths; here and there a morbid fruit fleshing at a rigid angle from the spike. "I wouldn't smell them too closely, if I were you."

Voltaire's smile, under his moustache and beard, was disgustingly superior: "I had already apprehended that, *mon ami.*"

"*Did* you?" said Tono in ready admiration. "I didn't. Not till I found out."

"My species has been given, *grâce à Chien*, enough instinct to keep the nose from the thorn."

"You're not a dachshund like the rest of us, are you?"

This time Voltaire yielded to joy, by all but

the very last tendril of scepticism. *("Pas vrai,"* he still kept on mechanically assuring himself. *"Calme-toi, Voltaire, mon ami ... Non, non, calme-toi, je t'en prie. Pas vrai du tout!")*

"You live very isolated and out-of-the-world here, is it not? There is not much social life? Not much *va-et-vient?* not much visiting?"

Tono was afraid, by this question, that his new friend would find it dull staying at the Villa Arabesque. Yet he could not in honesty contradict him.

"We *are* rather isolated on this headland," he confessed. "In fact, I don't really know of any other kennels in the neighbourhood; and, if there were, I'm not sure if the Legs would allow us any sort of social life of the kind no doubt you're used to in Paris. But even if we're a stay-at-home community, we find plenty to do, as you'll realise when you meet the other dachshunds."

"Ah-h-h!" Voltaire shivered again with the same secret ecstasy. And covered it by the sage remark: *"En effet,* one must cultivate one's garden."

"Well, candidly speaking, we don't actually cultivate it ourselves; we leave that to the Legs."

"How is the *cuisine* here?"

Tono thought this a funny question, but obligingly answered in detail: "Oh, a large and airy room, very agreeable, with a red-tiled floor and a vine at the windows and a multitude of omelette pans—"

"No, no, no"—impatiently. "I meant the cooking?"

Tono winced. "I have my dinner raw," he whispered, and turned his head away.

Voltaire was sorry. He took refuge in an aphorism: "It occurred to me, at one of your so British dinner parties in Paris, that the English have a hundred religions and only one sauce."

"But isn't one enough?"

"*Mais, mon pauvre—*"

At this juncture Tono interrupted by a hasty *detour* off the terrace and into the misty pewter sunlight of a grove of olives, because he had heard Fafnir and Wotan dodging about in the rubbery mesembryanthemum above the wall, and trying to get sight of the stranger dog without themselves being seen: "*Ach du*, Wotan, see, he has moustaches and a beard *and side-whiskers too!*" The discovery was followed by urchin guffaws.

("If Elsa spent less time in the kitchen, and more in improving their manners . . ." reflected Tono.) To distract the visitor's attention, he said:

"I wanted you to see our goldfish—" and hurried him along to a small shallow rock-pool, where the grass was long and moist, and they were free from puppy intrusion.

Voltaire politely said that it was very pretty; and added under his breath: "Chocolate-box."

"'They've all dived under the weeds." Tono peered over the mossy rim. "I expect you frightened them. Now, if we loop round by the boundary fence, we shall get to the wild part. The Master Legs takes me up there every afternoon. Not the others, only me. I wonder—" Tono hesitated. He had often wondered whether this strenuous exercising apart from the rest of the dogs, was a sign that the Master Legs loved him more, or loved him less?

"Continue"—politely from the griffon.

"You must have so much more opportunity, being a Parisian, to have studied the Legs'

"They've all dived under the weeds."

nature and what goes on in their minds—"

"I beg of you"—Voltaire spoke a little snappishly—"that you will not let it obsess you that I live in Paris. For one thing, I am really Belgian, not French. I was born outside Brussels—"

"So was I," said Tono with simple truthfulness. For though he had no idea of his birthplace, he was sure it could not have been *inside* Brussels.

"—And Legs are Legs, wherever you go, though recently we have travelled in Germany, and there, *parbleu*, I should speak of them as— what is your word—*trottères.*" Voltaire's lip curled. "But you are not interested in the politics. I will not weary you. You were going to confide in me perhaps something which you do not tell to the *other* dachshunds?"

The merest soupçon of derision in Voltaire's voice decided Tono to be a reticent little dog and keep his secret.

"This isn't the usual approach to the big swimming-pool. We're coming to it from the top," and he ran ahead down an open slope aromatic with rock myrtle, cistus and sweet-scented wild thyme. "You must get Erda to gather you a nosegay. I'm no botanist; but Erda is the nature-lover of our little family. Do you know"—Tono's eyes opened wide as he turned them full on Voltaire to see the effect of what he was going to say —"do you know, once she contributed a letter to the papers, saying 'Is this a record?'"

Voltaire asked was *what* a record? And Tono, surprised by such attention to detail, changed the subject but stuck to anecdote:

"We had a dog staying here for a little while, and we simply couldn't get him out of the swimming pool. He swam and swam and swam, all the time he was here. The Legs used to throw him a ball, and I barked and he swam, and then he brought it out in his mouth."

"And what did you do?"

"I went on barking," said Tono.

Voltaire suddenly resolved to make an experiment, and finally prove that his voluptuous conjecture was right:

"Was it a large dog?" he asked.

"Oh, an immense dog. They called him a cocker. And he was terribly clumsy, but that was because of his size. The Master Legs couldn't bear him."

Tono pranced with pleasure at the recollection. "He said: 'Give me Tono.'"

An immense dog. The last tendril of scepticism snapped. Now Voltaire knew for certain. He felt faint and hungry with rapture.

CHAPTER FOUR

The door of the cupboard in the Supreme Legs' room stood a little ajar, for the Butler Legs was putting away a suit. The Supreme Legs lay in bed patiently enduring a feverish bout of influenza. Beside the bed stood Tono, full of sympathy, with solemn unwavering eyes fixed compassionately on the invalid. Tono had a most sympathetic nature and an unflinching sense of responsibility. Had the Master Legs been ill, one would have felt compelled to refuse all food until he should be well again ("Stuff and nonsense and sheer affectation," said Elsa), but when it was the Supreme Legs, one need not do more than keep him company. Tono had now kept him company in this fashion for over half an hour, till the Supreme Legs, in a high state of hysteria for once in his life, rang frantic bells, and asked piteously that Tono should be removed.

"Come on, old boy," laughed the Master Legs, and whistled him to follow.

For one startled second, leaving the room, Tono believed he caught a swinging glimpse of the Vision.

By the gates at the end of the drive, the Master Legs stopped to send Tono back to the villa. "No good, old boy, back you go. Sailing isn't your cup of tea."

Tono could not see why that need be assumed so easily: sailing, for all he knew of it, might definitely be his bone and biscuit. However, he had heard Elsa, for whom he had an exasperated respect, impress on the puppies that the three rules they needed to observe were obedience, obedience and yet again obedience . . . (Elsa talked like that).

So he turned reluctantly and went back up the avenue again, deciding that he would look for his friend Voltaire and ask that sagacious Belgian to explain to him why obedience was three rules instead of only one? And did Elsa know that she had repeated herself, or was she perhaps becoming a little senile?

Meanwhile, a glossy black slip with unnaturally bright eyes had twinkled out of the bushes and was pattering down the dusty road, far enough behind the Master Legs that he did not become aware of it. And, as Eva pattered along, she chanted softly: " 'Fortnightly passenger and cargo services from San Francisco via Honolulu and from Seattle and Vancouver to Japan and China. Nippon Yusen Kaisha Line . . .Anchor Line . . . Bibby Line . . ."

("My, look at that cute little dachs," said a passing American Legs. "She's alone. I wonder if she's lost?")

"British West Indies, visiting Antigua, St. Kitts, Barbados, Grenada, British Guiana . . . Ben Line to the Far East, the Philippines and

Japan. . . . A thousand miles up the Amazon without change of ship, to Portugal, Madeira, Brazil. . . . Informal travel in cargo ships, a unique way of seeing the world in comfort. . . . Sailings subject to alteration without notice calls Pernambuco and Bahia, omits Madeira. Trans-Pacific passenger agency via Panama Canal . . . Henderson Line . . . Cunard White Star . . . Fyffes Line. . . . All sailings recognised by the Indian Government . . . twin-screw oil-driven mail. . . . Messageries Maritimes. . . . Messageries Maritimes. . . .

The Master Legs stood on the quay and signalled across the bay. From a small yacht, lifting and falling softly in the melting blue water, a dinghy put in towards the shore, quickly rowed by a deft-looking youth in a striped singlet and navy trousers. Eva, trembling with excitement, still had the prudence to dodge out of sight behind a couple of barrels until the dinghy was alongside and the Master Legs had sprung in. Then she ran forward eagerly, throwing a blue-black shadow on the brilliant sun-baked stone.

"My God, it's Eva! Hi! Stop! Wait a minute, Pierre. Look what we've got here."

Eva stood poised on the extreme edge of the stone, every nerve and muscle tense, pointing towards the horizon. Would her ruse succeed? Would he see, would he *see* what she wanted? The Legs were so dense.

"I'm not going home now for any bitch," exclaimed the Master Legs crossly. He looked round for somebody who might carry Eva back to the villa half a mile distant, but the little harbour was never much frequented, and now not a soul was in sight.

"You'll have to come along, my girl, and lump it ! That'll teach you not to do it a second time."

Pierre held on to a chain, while the Master Legs reached up to Eva, caught hold of her by her keel, and lifted her down into the rocking dinghy. Then they shot out towards the yacht.

Elsa, for once in a gracious maternal mood, was lying on the terrace in the late afternoon, with Fafnir and Wotan beside her, telling them some of those happy little German fairy-tales which were left over in her system from her distinguished ancestress, Thusnelda. Thus all Elsa's families could prattle very touchingly of Christmas trees, snow in the Black Forest, gingerbread, Nuremberg, *Stille Nacht, Heilige Nacht,* kobolds, and dear, dear Andersen and dear brothers Grimm.

Voltaire, curled into a circle nearby, listened with a deeply sardonic expression. Tono also listened, though his expression was far from sardonic, for these old-fashioned tales were just to his taste; and, when his own world was awry, he liked to hear of goodness and love being rewarded; and of all the useful little birds and animals, foxes and starlings and frogs, who scampered about and were of the greatest possible assistance to the Legs in their dauntless courage and their curious absence of any bump of locality. But his favourite was "The Ugly Duckling"; and when Elsa now came to the end of "The Mouse, the Bird, and the Sausage," he begged her to tell that one next. He added in an aside to Voltaire: "He grows into a swan, you know. He was clumsy and often in trouble and they didn't love him the same as they did the others, but he grew into a swan." And Voltaire, who could read Tono like a book, replied dryly: "It would seem to *me*, *mon petit*, that you had finished growing."

"More, *Muttichen*, more," clamoured the twin dachshunds. "Not 'The Ugly Duckling'; 'The Tinder-box.'"

Elsa chid them for their impatience, and asked where Erda was, and Eva? "Perhaps they would like to hear the *Märchen* as well as you." But Erda was with the Supreme Legs, lying devotedly on the bed, hardly breathing for fear she might disturb him; and none of them had seen Eva since the morning.

Elsa told the Grimm stories of "Hansel and Gretel," and "The Nose-Tree":

" . . . he gave her a whole pear to eat, and the nose came right. And as for the doctor, he put on the cloak, wished the king and his court a good day, and was soon with his two brothers; who lived from that time happily at home in their palace, except when they took an airing to see the world, in their coach with the three dapple-grey horses."

In the satisfied pause which succeeded the fairy tale and its mellow ending, when the sunset light along the eucalyptus bark and on the little dachshunds' coats and forepaws all blended into a warm golden hue of gingerbread, Voltaire remarked bitterly: "You would find a different Germany now, *chère* Elsa."

Elsa lifted her ears quickly at his tone: "Different? Why?"

Voltaire gave no direct answer.

"When were you there?" Elsa persisted.

"We visited Germany last autumn."

"Well?"

"Wood-cutters and charcoal-burners, goose-girls, kings and thumblings, huntsmen, brave little tailors, Christmas carols, spinning-wheels and chocolate houses in the forest—" Voltaire laughed; and then quoted:

" . . . lived from that time happily at home in their palace, except when they took an airing to see the world in their coach with the three dapple-grey horses."

"Well?" said Elsa again, made more uneasy by his laughter.

"Teach your puppies that it is now a steel Germany, with roads of steel. When you stop the car and ask the route, the young German-

Legs will point straight ahead and say with a triumphant shout in his voice: *'Grad'aus, nur grad'aus.'*

"Straight on," translated Elsa, for Tono's benefit.

But Tono was deeply puzzled to account for the sinister implication given to the chant by Voltaire, who was usually so detached.

Quite suddenly the griffon got up and walked away; up the steps to where the evening sun was hottest on the stone; and, shivering from some inner excitement, presently fell asleep; but went on shivering, and murmured mechanically two or three times:

"Vive la Belgique" and *"Nous sommes trahis,"* and sang a few bars of the *Brabançonne* in a cracked voice. . . .

Tono remarked to Elsa: "Isn't he behaving funny? I don't see what's wrong about telling a traveller to go straight on. It would be very misleading to say anything else, if it *was* straight on."

"French dogs are often like that." Elsa wrinkled her brows sagely. "I knew a French poodle once. I think I may say I knew him *very* well; in fact—" She stopped, for the puppies were still listening.

"Go on," said Tono. "In fact, what?"

"In fact I knew him very well," finished Elsa lamely. "One of his ancestors, he told me, had had a Legs who had fought in a war, and he did not feel fairy-tale about Germany, either."

"What was the war about?"

"Quarantine," said Elsa sharply. "All wars are about quarantine. Didn't you know?"

At that moment, when Tono was making a careful mental note to ask Voltaire what was quarantine, the twins sprang to their paws and waddled forward yelping: "Eva! Here's Eva.

Eva, where have you been? Why didn't you take us?"

A curious change had come over Eva. She rolled a little in her walk, and her eyes had that hard-bitten look which can come only from gazing at far horizons. She flumped down beside Elsa, and laid her nose along her paws without a word.

"It wouldn't do any harm to mention it," Elsa remarked sharply, "when you're going off for the whole day like that. Really, Eva, you use my kennel like a hotel. And what's that on your coat?" Elsa licked it roughly as the best way of finding out: "Salt! Now how in the world did you manage to get salt on your coat?"

After that, Eva was always being taken off to sea, and sometimes did not return to the villa for several days, even though the Master Legs himself came back. Tono heard him say to the Supreme Legs that she had the real Elizabethan seafaring spirit, and was no nuisance at all once they had set sail; the best of company, whether in calm weather or in a storm. She had found her sea-paws as though by magic;

and clung to the rigging and whined so piteously whenever he tried to land her, that he had left her to sleep on board with the Sailor Legs who adored her.

"And does she adore him?" asked the Relative Legs. "Aren't you jealous?"

"I needn't be. It's the boat she cares for, much more than for Pierre or me. I believe she'd sleep there alone when we're in harbour, and not mind a bit."

The Master Legs was wrong. True, Eva had taken little notice of him in the past, for she was not the temperament of dachshund that lay about among the Legs' legs. But since she had seen him at sea, managing a boat, cool and competent in mishap or dirty weather, dauntless at the helm, with debonair ease tacking or jibing or reefing as the wind demanded, she yielded up the independence of soul which had hitherto been her dearest possession, and secretly worshipped him, her hero of the Mediterranean headlands.

Tono may have seen past her jaunty airs, and suspected as much. But, even without that extra twist, he suffered agonies of jealousy at the mere notion of what propinquity might achieve for Eva. Eva went to sea with the Master Legs and spent whole days alone in his company. He struggled nobly, telling himself that all Legs should be free, and no dog could really hope to *own* a Legs. But self-argument did not help. The Master Legs used to be *his*.

Oh, why had not he, Tono, thought of following him down to the quay that day, and insisted on being taken aboard? He had no desire to go to sea *qua* sea, but a hopeless yearning to be a boon companion to his beloved Master Legs, morning, noon and night.

However, he did succeed in one innovation to his advantage. Hitherto he had slept in the hall, on a rug at the foot of the broad marble staircase. Elsa and the puppies, and Eva when she was at home, slept in luxurious kennels; and Voltaire, to the Relative Legs' annoyance, had coolly selected a spare kennel next to them for his sleeping quarters. Erda, of course, slept faithfully at the end of the Supreme Legs' bed, stretched across his feet.

"But why," reflected Tono, stunned by the

magnitude of the thought (he was often stunned by the magnitude of his thoughts), "why shouldn't I sleep in the same way, across the feet of my Master Legs? What possible objection could there be?"

He put it to Voltaire, whose eyes twinkled at some wicked joke: "If, of your own will, you spring upon the bed and lie across his feet, you will see, he will be delighted. It is simply that he has not had the idea himself."

So Tono began to agitate; and almost, though not quite, achieved his purpose. For some elusive reason, the Master Legs was a little bit stand-offish about having his little Tono actually across his feet; and threw him off at each attempt, sometimes forty-nine times in one night. But he most graciously, most kindly, most lovingly allowed him to sleep on the bed when he was away, and on the ground beside his bed when he was there.

Tono, having gained this much, managed to persuade himself that it was a big win over Eva, who had never slept in an upstairs bedroom at all; surely it meant that the Master Legs cared for him most? Essentially humble, the slightest extra notice went to his head; so now he began to give himself airs and be fussy over the whole procedure.

"I have the responsibility of putting Tono to bed tonight," said the Supreme Legs to his sister; for the yacht had departed on a three days' voyage, and of course Eva with it. She had expressed her hope, as she barked her good-byes and swaggered off, that they might put in at Hong Kong and Rio; and promised Fafnir to bring him back a bum freezer; not Wotan, who had angered her by calling out that if she showed her nose inside Hong Kong, she would find herself in the soup.

"*Put* him to bed?" demanded the Relative Legs. "What do you mean: 'put him'? Can't he just lie down like the rest of us?"

Apparently not. First, Tono had to be given his run: along the path to the left, pause near the garage, and then up the steps where the big acacia throws a feathery shadow, round again by the terrace where the bougainvillea is sharply scissored in small purple leaves against the side of the villa, two tall admonitory cypresses guarding a square of night-blue Mediterranean— But Tono turned his back on the Mediterranean and wished it were at the bottom of the sea.

"And now," said the Supreme Legs, in measured tolerance of the order of things, as he opened the door into the Master Legs' room and courteously stood aside for Tono to go in first, "now we strip back the cover because Tono doesn't like to lie on satin—"

Tono leapt on the bed.

"—And now we switch off the lights, all except this one lamp; only I must pull down the shade so that it doesn't shine in his eyes and keep him awake; but he doesn't like to be left completely in the dark. We close the windows so that Tono shouldn't be cold but we leave this one a little open, or Tono would find it too stuffy. Good night, Tono. And now the door not quite shut, so that in case he gets claustrophobia in the night—Tono has a slight tendency to claustrophobia—he must know that he is able, if he wants to, to get out of the room and walk about the corridors. And now I think that's all."

"Are you sure?" interposed the Relative

Legs. "Wouldn't he like me to sit by him for a bit, and read him a psalm?"

Tono hoped she would not do anything of the sort. It was kind of her to offer. Very kind and thoughtful. But he preferred at this juncture to be left alone to his meditations. Besides, he was afraid he might yawn, and the Legs were apt to be so touchy when you yawned at them.

His meditations were profoundly unhappy. This was the first time, since Eva had become a seafaring bitch, that she and the Master Legs had both been away from the villa all night. And when the next night and the next did not see their return, he became so mournful that the other dogs eschewed his company.

And so it happened that he was lying solitary on the terrace of the cypresses, his back to the sea, when Eva returned, rolling more than ever in her walk and humming that fine old sea-shanty: "Whisky Johnny":

"Oh, whisky is the life of man—"

Tono was shocked. He decided to speak

seriously to this poor misguided puppy, for her own good.

"It's only your good that I care about," he informed Eva; which was not a wholly accurate rendering of the more complicated movements in his psychology, but of these he was not aware. "It's no life for a well-bred bitch from a good kennel, knocking about with a lot of rough dogs."

"There aren't any dogs at sea, only fish." Eva remained quite impenitent.

"There are dogfish, aren't there?"

"Poor Tono!"

"Eva," he went on heavily, "you'll get your bloom knocked off. You know what value the Legs set on your bloom."

"Come out of the lee scuppers," laughed Eva. "They mean the bloom of my coat, not my morals."

"And that disgusting song you were sing-ing."

"The Master Legs taught it to me."

This was a sword in Tono's heart, but he dissembled, and prosed on: "Elsa is very gravely concerned about you." (Elsa at that very moment was squatting beside the Chef Legs, her eyes yearning upwards, her attitude betokening that here was a poor little mendicant dachshund who had been starved for years but at long last sees a slender chance of food, and pours her whole being into one bald, naked, shameless concentration-point above her head.)

"Shiver my timbers!" exclaimed Eva suddenly. "The wind's changed; it's SE by E now, so we should make an early start to-morrow. I must be off to get some sleep."

Even when she was out of sight, Tono still heard, carried on the fresher breeze:

> *"Roll down—roll down to Rio—*
> *Roll really down to Rio!*
> *Oh, I'd love to roll to Rio*
> *Some day before I'm old!"*

CHAPTER FIVE

No one had ever told Tono that it was of little use attempting to copy something, which another person had just successfully pulled off. By his simple process of logic, Eva's exploit was direct proof that what the Master Legs *liked* was for a little dog to follow him, without being seen, as far as the harbour; and at the critical moment to stand on the edge of the wharf and with a sharp, intelligent bark communicate the desire to be taken along, and so become for ever afterwards the Master Legs' good companion of the seas.

If, argued Tono to himself, he carried out these directions which Eva had unwittingly given him, meticulous not to depart from the slightest detail in the chain of events, his days and nights of jealousy would soon lie as far in the past as the hastening clouds quitting the sky and leaving it brilliant azure from the hills to the horizon.

A pity, perhaps, that he did not consult Voltaire over his plan. Voltaire, for all his twisted humour, his joy in life's ironic spectacle, might well have been decent enough to discourage Tono from imitating Eva, without, so to speak, Eva's equipment.

So the very next time Eva and the Master Legs went off to the yacht, Tono, keeping a fair distance behind, his heart thumping heavily till he felt it would burst his ribs, ran the half-mile downhill to the quay, busier today, with a couple of fishing boats setting their burnt-orange sails to catch the brisk wind. Crouching behind a heap of lobster baskets, he watched the dinghy row in from the yacht which was anchored a few hundred yards outside the harbour. The steps were occupied by the men unloading wood, so the little boat pulled in where the stone wall ran steeply down to the water, and the young Sailor Legs held on to an iron ring while the Master Legs lifted Eva and handed her down to him, and then sprang in himself. This, according to schedule, was Tono's moment. He ran forward to the edge of the quay just above them, and stood there, silhouetted and expectant, calling attention to his presence with an exultant bark.

The Master Legs looked up. And from that moment the situation departed from the pattern previously laid out by Eva, and plunged into a confused and terrifying design of its own.

"Oh, hell" exclaimed the Master Legs. Then emphatically: "Go home, Tono. Bad dog! Go *home*, sir! *Holà*, Jean-Marie"—calling out in French to a Fisher Legs less occupied than the rest—"my dog's followed me down here. Can you take him up to the Villa Arabesque?"

The Fisher Legs moved towards Tono. Tono, thinking mistakenly that this was still an occasion for initiative and enterprise, and quite resolved that once he was aboard the yacht all would be well, leapt from the five-foot wall into the dinghy.

The dinghy all but capsized. It rocked violently from side to side. The Master Legs swore. Eva yelped. The water rushed in over the side. Tono, terrified, lurched, scrambled, lost his footing and fell overboard, fortunately not far from the steps. Bewildered, the water singing in his ears and blinding his eyes, he swam madly in several different directions at once, till two or three Fisher Legs, with roars of rough laughter and derision, lugged him ashore by the collar, while water poured from him over their espadrilles, and he stood miserably shivering, and wondering why the same adventure had ended in such triumph for Eva, such a fiasco for him.

All he cared for now was to be carried home in the arms of the Master Legs, with comforting words and the promise that he should be taken for a nice sail tomorrow.

But the Master Legs was angry, for he hated his spruce little dinghy to be slopping over from having shipped half the Mediterranean; and hated, moreover, changing his arrangements once they were made. So he ordered the Sailor Legs to bale it out, and then row back with Eva to the yacht, while he himself ran Tono uphill very quickly on a lead, leaving a trail of water dark in the dust to mark their passage; led him straight to the stables, and with a rough, prickly towel gave him a rub-down which was all efficiency and none of it tenderness, telling him the while what he thought of his bad behaviour. Then, as Tono, even when dry, seemed unable to stop trembling from the nervous shock of his immersion, he was given, not raw meat for once, but a large bowl of hot milk with a very curious taste in it from something that the Master Legs had lavishly poured from a flask.

"Lie down now and go to sleep," he said sternly, and strode away, closing the door behind him.

Tono crouched down into the straw. He could not sleep; his brain was hot and snapping. Presently the warm, shadowy darkness surrounding him began to move, to tilt and sway like a boat; and the setting sun, which crept in at the chinks and slits, and lay in a soft but brilliant pattern on the straw, also began to move and caper. It was all very strange. And Tono was glad when Erda's deeply sympathetic black nose showed under the lift of the door, and Erda herself, flattened into the shape of a supple black pancake, followed her nose and scrabbled into the stable beside him. She had heard the Master Legs tell the Supreme Legs the story of Tono's mishap and disgrace, and Erda's heart was soft and dark and fragrant as mushrooms on toast. She grieved for Tono. She went to look for him that she might share his exile for an hour or two. When he sobbed, she sobbed quite easily as well.

"It isn't that I don't love the Master Legs," wept Tono. "I'd like to die for him—"

"—So would I," chimed in Erda, thinking of the Supreme Legs. "I'd like to die for *him.*"

The walls and the sunlit straw see-sawed to a more extravagant rhythm. Tono lapped up the last of the hot milk with its queer luscious taste.

"And I want no reward. There he is—I mean there he would be—dying—"

"In the snow," whispered Erda.

"—Dying in the snow: 'Who is this coming towards me in my hour of need? Why, it's Tono!'"

"'Why, it's Erda!'" whispered Erda along her own thread. " 'Yes, it's your little Erda who loves you best!'"

"'It's *Tono*,'" obstinately. "'Brave Tono, whom I have never valued sufficiently, and with a barrel of brandy round his neck. Lo! I am saved.'"

Erda, always responsive, was powerfully affected.

"There, there," said Tono, flinging his paw across her neck.

Erda explained that it was so dreadful to think of the Supreme Legs so nearly dying like that in the snow. Tono had to disillusion her: it was not the Supreme Legs at all, it was the Master Legs. Erda was sweet and pretty, but she was a little slow in the uptake:

"There aren't any opportunities of saving a Legs' life," Tono complained fretfully. "They hardly ever run into danger. There's fire, of course, and drowning. And if they were attacked by a homicidal maniac, one could worry the homicidal maniac's ankles. But these chances are getting rarer and rarer. It's all speedboats and flying nowadays," he finished, and wept anew. "I'm not a dog that shows his feelings much," he rambled on, half to her, half in the air. "I do my duty and I want no reward." Suddenly he became truculent, and glared at Erda so that she shrank back. "I told you, didn't I, that I wanted no reward? Well, I want no reward. Oh, Erda"—melting into a fresh maudlin orgy—"I do love him so terribly."

"So do I love him terribly. Oh, Tono!"

"Then you should con-control yourself," Tono enjoined her loftily. "You're too shentimental, Erda. It'll get you into trouble. Erda"—sleepily—"Erda. And you too, Erda. Listen, both of you. I've never told this to any dog before."

"Oh, tell me," she cried eagerly. "Please do."

By now Tono was feeling relaxed and almost happy. Quite happy, in fact. It seemed to him that this was no bad way of spending a day: just to lie there in a muzziness of dusk and hot

milk and confidences. What had happened ear-
lier in the day hardly mattered, nor what would
happen tomorrow. Really, Eva was rather silly
and over important, strutting about on four
paws as though she owned the Seven Seas:
"Erda, what's four times seven?"

Erda did not know.

"Never mind." It did not matter. *He* was
the privileged one, not Eva. He had seen Dog.
But it was wholly essential that Erda, at least,
should understand his splendour, and understand he had been thus privileged.

"You mustn't tell," anxiously.

"No, no, no, I promise."

"Not the twins, nor Eva, nor Elsa, nor Voltaire."

"Not one of them."

"Nor Erda. Promise you won't tell Erda?"

Erda was puzzled, but she thought she had better promise that, too.

"Because, you see, I particularly want them all to know."

"You mean you particularly *don't* want them all to know?"

"I particularly do. I particularly don't. Promise you'll tell every one of them?" Wildly, Erda promised.

"Erda"—in solemn tones—"I've seen a vision of Dog. It was one moonlit night. . ."

CHAPTER SIX

ERDA REMAINED, not unnaturally, in a state of utter bewilderment. She had solemnly promised to tell; she had solemnly promised not to tell. This was not the sort of problem one could take to one's mother; besides, Elsa had one of her concentrated kitchen periods, and would not be interested. Nor did Erda like the idea of approaching Tono anew and asking him to solve the riddle, for Tono was going about the next day with a glazed expression in his eyes, and turning his head slightly away from everybody. His understanding of events that had happened seemed to be limited and thick.

Then Erda caught sight of their visiting dog, Voltaire, gravely employed in removing a deeply embedded tick from an almost inaccessible patch of his anatomy. Every now and then he fell over sideways. Voltaire, Erda remembered, was a sage and a philosopher. She trotted up to the fourth grass terrace, the one below the cactus garden and above the rows of orange trees, and, with many pretty hesitations, apologised for disturbing him at his work.

"Not at all. I like little puppies to come to me with their troubles. Go on, my dear."

"Do you believe in miracles?"

"I have never seen a greater miracle in the world than myself."

"Of course," Erda politely agreed. And then she told him how Tono had seen a vision of Great Dog through a hole in the wall of the inner courtyard.

The effect of this on the middle-aged cynic was beyond anything Erda could have conceived. At first incredulous, Voltaire suddenly went off into an ecstasy. His eyes dilated till they reminded Erda of the Dog with Eyes as Large as Windmills, in one of her mother's fairy-stories. He fell off the wall on to the terrace below; he rolled on his back; he kicked his paws into the air, wheezing and choking, the tears streaming.

When he could calm himself sufficiently, he enjoined Erda never to mention to Tono that she had betrayed one of her promises.

"But won't he ask me?"

"*Mais non,*" said Voltaire. "Between you and me and the lamp-post, as they say in England, he has forgotten yesterday. They do."

"He's so queer this morning. He was queer last night, too, but in a different way. He keeps brushing his paw across his eyes as though to rub away something in front of them, only there's nothing there; and if one barks anywhere close to him, he starts and moans. And he's drunk up all the water in his own bowl, and ours too. Now he's drinking the swimming pool."

"What he wants, but he does not know it, is the hair of the Legs that bit him. Run away, *ma petite*, and find a nice bone to play with and think no more about the matter."

"Voltaire, isn't it wonderful to think that Great Dog should actually appear in our own villa to our own Tono?"

Voltaire liked this innocent, beautiful puppy. She reminded him of things he had almost forgotten in his own puppyhood; and she reminded him of flowers, too; of the velvet petals of a pansy, of the bloom on a plum. He sighed after she had left him, but he could not be regretful for long. He had been a gay Legs in his youth, taking life lightly as a passing affair which need involve no responsibilities: out of a hundred passions a year, he could rarely remember more than two; usually none. Once, certainly, his heart had been broken: an exquisite little Pekinese bitch, the colour of sunflowers, daffodils, and cream.... Yes, she had played fast and loose with his affections, and finally, under his very nose, had married her uncle in a restaurant in the Bois de Boulogne. He had recovered from all that, and no bitch alive (he hoped) had the power to stir him. When you are ten years old, *ma foi*, you should be exempt from turmoil, desire, and the pains of rivalry. When you are ten years old, you should settle down to find a detached pleasure and occupation in the absurdities of other dogs: " 'A wise dog,'" Voltaire quoted (much too often) " 'never loses anything if he has himself.'"

But never had he encountered such a deliciously grotesque pantomime as here in this remote villa in the Midi, where he had consented to be brought simply because he thought a little sunshine during the spring months might be good for his rheumatism; and was rewarded by the spectacle of Tono, a victim of surely the most extraordinary delusion in the whole history of dog.

Yet the little dachshunds who were not inside the ring of delusion had never mentioned to him what was so palpable? Why not?

Voltaire puzzled over this, but not for long. With a shrug of the shoulders, he decided that they took the normal for granted, and it had therefore never occurred to them how Tono's brain could have conceived anything so fantastic. Besides, only Elsa was mentally capable of such speculations, and she must long ago have decided against *la vie contemplative* *i*n favour of *la vie gourmande.*

Voltaire rose and trotted up to the swimming pool, where he assumed he would find Tono still quenching his unquenchable thirst. And, indeed, there he was. It was a grey day, and there were no reflections. The griffon hailed him with exasperating cheerfulness: "Ah, *le voici.* Good day, sweet Prince."

Tono stopped lapping, lifted his head, and stared at Voltaire out of heavy, bloodshot eyes.

"Who's sweet prince?"

"Hamlet."

"Who's Hamlet?"

"A Dane."

"Then why do you call *me* 'sweet prince'?"

"Because,'" replied Voltaire in dulcet tones, "because I am so exceedingly whimsical."

Tono sighed, and gave it up. He was not deeply interested. "Tell me," he began, and flumped on the marble beside his friend.

"*Et bien, mon ami,* what shall I tell you?" Voltaire's voice wooed for confidences.

"You must have noticed—" Tono stopped again.

"I notice little," said Voltaire, concealing his impatience at the slow progress. "I notice little and guess nothing. Over words I am stupid. You must explain, you who have the gift of eloquence."

Tono, encouraged, though he did not feel eloquent this morning, rather as though a palsied paw had to go out and fumble for every thought, began: "You've seen all over the villa, and even here on the steps coming up to the pool, all those statues and things?"

"I have remarked them, yes." He knew that Tono referred to the Tang Buddha carved in wood which squatted in a niche in the hall, wisely brooding over the destinies of the Villa Arabesque, and that other smaller bronze Buddha that confronted you from the top of a *barguegno* in the upper patio as you came up the staircase; and those Immortals, two from a set of eight of the best period of Kanghsi which reigned on either side of the sitting-room fireplace. And to the Chinese goddess, Kuan-yin, half-way up the staircase; and to St. Florian, protector against fire, who stood clad in armour just below where they lay, in the coign of the last flight of steps up to the swimming-pool. "The Legs call them their 'gods,'" said Voltaire.

"All of them?"

"Yes, all. 'They cannot make a worm, yet they will be making gods by dozens.'"

"And they worship them?"

"More or less."

"But—" Tono stopped again. It was heavy going, like a dray uphill over cobblestones. "But they look like the Legs themselves."

Voltaire replied, a whole under-tow of meaning in his voice: "The Legs make their gods in their own image."

"But don't they want them larger than their own image? At least ten times as large? I should have thought-" he fumbled and was silent.

Voltaire gave a queer little dry chuckle. Undoubtedly he was tickled to death. Yet he eyed Tono with a sort of compassion mixed with his amusement, began to say something and then decided against it. A shame to spoil a situation so exquisitely ludicrous; which had, moreover, only himself to behold and appreciate it.

"Voltaire, you *do* believe in Dog, don't you?"

"*Mon pauvre ami!*"

"Well, but you do, don't you?"

"I am what they call a sceptic," said Voltaire slowly. "You must not let that trouble you."

Tono was troubled for an instant, but then he exulted in his secret proof. In fact, he felt sorry for Voltaire, who, for all his ripe wisdom and experience, had not been privileged to gaze upon Great Dog.

CHAPTER SEVEN

Eva was spending a couple of days ashore, though her manner made it clear to the rest of the dogs that she now regarded the villa merely as a convenient port in which to dock while the cross-head blocks were being lubricated and intermediate poppets fitted. She had gone through her novitiate when she had swaggered and used too much sea-slang and sailors' oaths, and was already at that second and even more exasperating stage of her ocean career when her very soul was pickled in brine; and she dissociated herself from a life on land except as some poor accessory to real life, glorious life; a life where you sailed goose-wing before the wind, watching the flight of a sea-gull, worrying and biting the tackle, curled up in the heart of a rope coil, rejoicing when the anchor had been weighed and they gathered way, free at last, she and the Master Legs and the Sailor Legs.

This sort of talk, while it bored Elsa, puzzled Erda, and worried Tono to death, was most of all maddening to her puppy brothers, who thought very properly that if anyone went to sea, it ought to be themselves and not the bitch of the basket.

"Stupid, conceited little thing," Fafnir declared privately to Wotan. "I don't believe she knows a parbuckle from a Double Matthew Walker."

Wotan agreed. Neither did he. But that was beside the point.

They became more and more discontented with mere garden adventures; playing hide-and-seek among the oleander-bushes seemed tame and poor-spirited compared with the thrill of easing up the mainsheet when the wind was fresh and topping up the mainsail, which Eva declared she did constantly and single-pawed.

"Tell that to the Kerry blues!" scoffed Fafnir, but with uneasy envy rippling down his whole stomach-length. And "Tell that to the Kerry blues!" echoed Wotan.

Eva laughed, and trotted away with a slight list to starboard.

Fafnir growled at her jaunty tail; at least, he meant it to be a growl, but actually it still came out as very much of a squeak. It was by mere accident that Eva had originally gone to sea and they had stayed at home; so he thought; belittling that ardent desire which had sent Drake to sea, and Raleigh, Columbus and Hudson; all that gallant company of which Eva was now one.

"*Du, Wotan, hör'mal*"—Elsa could not get them out of the habit of occasionally babbling German. Crouching flat under the bushes where the long grass hid them from the sight of any passing Legs, they plotted a plot which should result in the total discomfiture of Eva.

They had picked up information that the yacht was not anchored a little way off the land, but actually in harbour for repairs. So that it would be an easy matter, Fafnir argued in his infantile optimism, to slip down silently, flattening their way under bushes or close to the shadow of the walls, a few hours before the Master Legs was about to start on another voyage, and both ship before the mast. Wotan asked what was that? and Fafnir replied vaguely: "You know what a mast is, *nicht? Nu also*, we ship before it."

Choosing a moment when the Sailor Legs was at the estarninet, and no other Legs were about, they scuttled along the jetty, getting terribly tangled and scrumbled up with the nets spread out to dry; jumped on board without any difficulty, and hid themselves in the sail locker. So it came to pass that when the Master Legs and Eva and the Sailor Legs put out to sea, they actually had no notion that two valiant stowaways were aboard.

Twelve hours later, they were making an ignominious journey back to the villa; carried, squirming and dank, in a canvas bucket. Eva ran alongside the Master Legs, tumbling over herself with merriment. She could hardly wait to tell the other dogs about the gale; and how Fafnir and Wotan had been discovered, when out of sight of land, by their sick wails which rose even above the whistle of the freshening breeze; and how they had been sick almost the whole time without stopping; how they had been sick *in* the locker, and after they had been taken *out* of the locker; and how they had gone on being sick, and had wished to die, and had lain in sodden lengths with suffering ears and eyes closed, just wherever they were put; and could not get out of the way when sworn at or pushed by the Master Legs who had said: "One dachshund I'll put up with, if it's Eva. Three of you—hell, no!"

"What did they eat?" enquired Elsa.

"It isn't what they ate. It's what they un-ate!" Eva shook with the eternal heartless laughter of those who feel grand at sea, for those who don't feel the least bit hungry, thank you.

"I didn't know they had so much in them," she went on; which is what, but in an entirely different sense, the twins had hoped she would say after their maiden trip.

Erda, of course, mourned sympathetically over their humiliation: "You're so hard, Eva."

"Nonsense!" from the mother of all the dachshunds. "If you're not hard, you get trodden upon. And as for you, Erda, you're much too much of a doormat. You'd like the Supreme Legs to wipe his feet on you."

Erda sobbed a little. She would; she did; he had.

"And as for the twins, they're running wild and running silly. School is what they want. They should have been entered for Eton or Winchester long ago, and then we wouldn't have had all this yapping and yelping and stowawaying."

"Why weren't they?" asked Tono, literal as usual.

Elsa shrugged, and snapped at a fly: "That's their father's business, not mine."

Voltaire, always ready to draw out Elsa when she was in one of her rarely communicative moods, asked: "The twins and Eva, did they have the same father as Erda?"

"I don't know replied Elsa coldly. She shoved her nose down between her paws and growled something which sounded like (but could not have been): "Ad 'is 'at on at the time."

But Voltaire persisted: "*Dites donc*, Elsa, what is the number of families you have had in your six years?"

Elsa, still vague, said it might have been nine or it might have been eight; she really couldn't be expected to remember and she really couldn't see that it was of any interest to any inquisitive Frenchies who concerned themselves too much about certain things and not nearly enough about others.

Eva broke in, still over-excited from the storm.

"The Master Legs is terribly pleased with me because I enjoy dirty weather. He enjoys it too. He called me 'Grace Darling.'"

Tono winced sharply. So he called her "darling," even in the midst of peril at sea. Did he ever call Tono "darling"? No, never.

"Were you wrecked on an island?" Erda asked, "And were there flowers, and did you pick some and twine them in the ropes when you sailed away again? I think they'd look so pretty, stuck in the ropes."

"Sheets," Eva brightly corrected her.

Erda's only acquaintance of sheets were those that she snuggled under on cold nights in the blessed bed of the Supreme Legs. But the nights now at the end of May were rapidly getting warmer, and last week the worst had happened: he had very gently lifted her from inside the bed and put her outside it, where she could not snuggle, and told her that summer had come.

. . . A deep sigh from Elsa seemed to Erda but an echo of her own melancholy. Elsa had been thinking of Sieglinde, as she always did when any tactless dog touched on the subject of her past. Sieglinde . . . "Was she the same family as Lohengrin, I wonder?" musing half aloud. "No, I think she was two or three families after. One forgets." Yes, she remembered now: Sieglinde was one of the litter she had had in the cabin-trunk left half packed for the Legs to go to England.

"Erda isn't a patch on her," Elsa suddenly exclaimed aloud fiercely, and she shifted her head and stared without blinking at Tono, who shifted a little uncomfortably and wondered what he had done wrong.

Voltaire yawned, a capacious yawn. The conversation was not amusing any more: it was sentimental and domestic.

"Do you ever hear from her?"

"No, she never writes. You know what daughters are, once they leave the home kennel."

"*Grâce à Chien*, I do not know what daughters are. And what should make me even more thankful, *chère* Elsa, I do not know where they are. Nor do we know, any of us," he went on, his eyes goggling appreciation of his own tirade, "where our next daughters are coming from. I have made it my motto, I, and it is a motto more especially appropriate to your breed than to mine, never to let my front paws know what my back paws doeth. Or, in other words, the words of an English minor poet: 'One heat, all know, doth drive out another.'"

"I want some water," Elsa cut in abruptly. She could not bear him any longer in that mood. She got up and waddled away. She was humming: "*Ich weiss nicht was soll es bedeuten, das sich so traurig bin . . .*"

CHAPTER EIGHT

UNFAMILIAR STEPS! Visitors! Strangers! Alert, the dogs sprang up from the terrace with loud resentful barking. So, metaphorically, did the Legs. They did not care for uninvited visitors, either. Nor did the Butler Legs, decorous in white linen. But she passed him at a little run; and under her arm, by Sirius, she was carrying a female dog, who wore an emerald green collar with little silver bells.

"Nong, sill voo play, let me announce myself. I can't be formal. I simply can't." And then, addressing herself to the Supreme Legs: "The only way, when you're shy, is to be terribly natural, isn't it? and I really couldn't be more shy, though you wouldn't believe it to see me, would you now? And I simply had to come up, just to make friends. There, now it's out! You see, we're neighbours, and—oh, those dogs! What darlings! What petsies! I do adore dachshunds, the roly-poly-olies—Eeeh!"—a scream of terror as she suddenly caught sight of Tono. He was barking away furiously with the other dachshunds, but merely as a matter of form; he did not actually feel antagonistic; so he was rather hurt at being singled out by these preposterous stranger Legs. "I'se vewy, vewy fwightened!" She backed behind the Master Legs.

"He's all right," he assured her. "Down, Tono! Good dog! Quiet!"

"Ooh, I'se scared, and so's Dulcibel. Does he bite?"

Well, *really*, thought Tono.

Very cautiously, on being further reassured

as to Tono's amiability (she was not bothering about the other dachshunds, nor about the griffon), she lowered Dulcibel to the ground. Dulcibel, on high mean legs like sticks, immediately sidled towards Voltaire and lay down beside him. She had not one point which was not common and frightful, yet the dogs of the villa had to admit, nevertheless, that there was something faintly attractive, faintly dangerous, in her personality.

It was obvious that the Supreme Legs felt the same thing, when he asked Dulcibel's Legs in a low voice whether . . . ? And she cried: "Oh *no*, not for *weeks* yet!."

She wore white satin trousers with a light blue stripe, and further up (where somehow Tono saw better than the others) a frogged pink *crêpe-de-Chine* shirt, and a light-blue scarf, and round her golden curls a silk handkerchief knotted Spanishly to one side, and over that, worn even more Spanishly on the other side of her head, a large white hat. The nails of the hand which had clasped Dulcibel were enamelled each one a different shade. Harlequin style. Amusin'.

The Master Legs went in to shake cock-
tails, while the Supreme Legs, who before she
came had been outstretched in the speckled
shade of the eucalyptus tree, quietly enjoying
his book, set himself to the task of entertaining
her; his tone taking on that deadly courtesy
which Elsa knew from experience meant that
at any moment something very firm and dis-
concerting might emerge. Elsa entirely agreed
with his opinion of the newcomer. She called
Eva and Erda to her side. The twins were listening fascinated to what the stranger had to
say about herself and her Legs; but the twins,
Elsa decided, were too young for a corrupt influence to matter. In six months, perhaps . . .

Erda obeyed the call immediately. Eva,
adoring life in all its more rakish and piratical
forms, and eager especially for novelty from
those wearisome days which occasionally she
and the Master Legs had to spend on shore,
pretended not to hear; and continued to remain
with Tono and Voltaire and the twins, who lay
in an absorbed ring and listened while the
voluble Dulcibel sprayed them with synthetic
charm:

"We're films, you see, only we're resting. Oh yes, both of us. I always say, when it's a question of my contract, 'No, I'm very sorry, but I wouldn't dream of accepting unless my Highly Insured Legs is included.' And, my dears, they usually give way. They're such worms, all these Studio Legs. Sometimes I feel quite tempted to give them a sharp nip in the trousers, and then I say to myself, 'No, Dulcibel, no, turn the other cheek and you won't regret it.' Yes, of course it's desperately hard work, but as long as I please my public . . . I mean, after all, now that Rin-tin-tin is dead, who *is* there? Oh, Asta and Scruffy, I know. But I mean . . . well, after all—though of course one mustn't be a cat—"

(From the cocktail group, further up the terrace, drifted the voice of the Highly Insured Legs: "I mean, now that Jean Harlow's dead, who is there? Oh, yes, I know there's Carole Lombard, but, after all . . . well, I *ask* you!")

"Oh, naturally, I'd rather be on the legit. My dream is to play Flush in the *Barretts.* They could easily write her up as a white Pomeranian. Of course my Legs isn't *quite* right for

Elizabeth Barrett, but one can't please everybody. And between ourselves, you know, at
times I do find her a bit of a drag. However,
fidelity and service, those are my watchwords.
But it's so difficult to get a footing. And then
there's Shakespeare. It's a pity, that he never
wrote a really good part for a bitch. There was
Launcelot Gobbo's dog, but that's very small
beer. I don't know how long we're staying here;
Korda is thinking of us for his next historical
epic, and we're just waiting to hear. And meanwhile we've been lent the Casetta Sans Gône,
about half a mile from here; but it's a lonely
spot and no intellectual society until now" (with
a coy flick of the tail towards Voltaire). "I expect, now the ice is broken, we shall be like one
big family. That last picture . . . all those re-
takes. . . . Hollywood is *so* exhausting—"

"Hollywood? Oh, have you *really*, really
been to California?"

"Of course," replied Dulcibel, smiling
kindly down at Eva's little black-and-tan muzzle
so eagerly lifted to hers. "I've been to California and Elstree and *everywhere.*"

"Did you go by the New Zealand Line?
Did you touch at Kingston? Did you go through

the Panama Canal? What does San Francisco look like from the Pacific?"

"East, west, kennel's best. Believe me, little one, what I yearn for most is my own cushion; it's shabby and the stuffing's a bit loose, but oh, so cosy! An old bone or two—I've no patience with dogs who have to have a fresh bone at every meal—and one day perhaps a lot of darling little puppies of my own."

"Good Dog!" ejaculated Eva in disgust.

"*Eva!*" Elsa called, for the tenth time.

"She's a little stand-offish, isn't she?" whispered Dulcibel to Voltaire. "Not that I take offence easily. I know there is still an old-world prejudice among pedigree dogs about going into films. I come of a long line of champions myself, so I know and I can understand—"

("Of course," chirruped the Highly Insured Legs, "I can't help realising that there's still an old-world prejudice against the films. I come of a very old Rutlandshire family myself, so I know and can understand, and I do assure you, and you must believe me, that I'm never so happy as when I'm just digging in my garden among my roses. Shall I tell you what Louis B. Mayer said to me the other day? 'Why,' he said, 'with all that genius, you're just a simple golden-hearted little girl.'")

" . . . never so happy as when digging in my garden," Dulcibel assured them. "You mustn't let my glamour and genius frighten you. Under it all, you'll find out that I'm just a simple golden-hearted little bitch. It's my temperament. When you're an art*ee*ste, you have temperament and it's no good trying to alter it; can the Dalmatian change his spots?"

Tono opened his eyes very wide, and pricked up his ears. "Spots?" he said. "Is that the same one that has the dog-cart?"

Dulcibel stared: "Pardon?" And waited for Tono to say "Granted as soon as asked," as they did in Rutlandshire. But he was too busy on the scent of this erratic thing called Dalmatian which lately had twice cropped up in the conversation. Somehow it intrigued him. It had spots and a dog-cart. What else had it? Could it change its spots? Could it change its dog-cart? And—Oh, well, never mind. Already, while he had been thus pondering, Dulcibel had let her little pink flannelette tongue run fluently on to other subjects. She turned to Voltaire and was declaring with emphasis: "I never did care for clean-shaven dogs. What I mean is, there's no *flavour* in an affair with a clean-shaven dog. Not that I have affairs in that light way. I fall in love, and I suffer, but I willingly accept suffering; it's necessary for my art: 'Love is of dog's life a thing apart, 'tis a bitch's whole existence!'"

Eva remarked that she thought they were all being absolutely horrid about their recent visitor. Horrid and snobbish; yes, and spiteful.

"You don't know what you're talking about, my *pupchen*," said Elsa, not unkindly. "We've so little social life here at the villa that how could you know if a dog is out of the Cruft drawer or not?"

"Perhaps she's not so bad," suggested Tono.

"She is a reeff-raff." Voltaire pronounced his verdict. "What is it happens when a pug and a white Pomeranian go out walking together? Yes? Answer me that."

"I can't." Tono was hopelessly out of his depth. "I was never any good at riddles." He sank his nose deep within his paws, and gazed at Voltaire for enlightenment. "What *does* happen?"

"Our new friend"—drily.

Elsa picked up the solution, which pleased her. *"Of course!* I'd been wondering. Pug and Pomeranian. That great white cotton ruff sticking out for miles; at least, off-white; not white. And her tail curled round and round and pressed flat against her back so that she couldn't wag it even if she tried."

"That is a happy dispensation, perhaps," said Voltaire. "Otherwise she would never stop. She is wagsome by nature, *cette petite affreuse.*"

"And the thin little staggery legs. Mostly Pomeranian. I should have recognised it at once, except for the sort of pug effect flattening her features as if somebody had sat on them."

"I expect a good many dogs have done so," Voltaire interrupted, enjoying the duet with rather more viciousness and less wit than was his wont; for he knew Dulcibel was sham and awful, *tout ce qu'il y a de plus ordinaire*, but nevertheless she had disturbed him; and Voltaire, at his age, resented even the slightest disturbance of this nature. He had boasted too often that he had renounced all forms of life but the Purely Intellectual.

Fafnir and Wotan came wriggling and frisking up to the group, with short sharp puppy bursts of enthusiasm: her voice! her nose! her tail! Ach, and her coat! Her coat, especially, was the loveliest they had ever seen; that shining silken ruff, pure white like a celestial Pierrette. This was not quite how they put it, but then the twins so far had a very limited vocabulary; hotly they vied with each other as to which of them she had looked at first or most or last. And they besought Tono, the most good-natured of their seniors, to get her autograph for them.

"Really," said Elsa. "Four puppies, and only one of them with any sense." And she glanced over to where Erda lay, peaceful and adoring, at the feet of the Supreme Legs. "I'm going to get a drink. I need it." And she went round the terrace towards the trough near the kitchen door. One day, she hoped, the puppies would realise in good earnest about the off-white Dulcibels of this world.

Voltaire closed his eyes and composed himself as though for sleep, though he was cynically aware that the days of his unbroken sleep were over.

"*'Souvent chienne varie.'*" he murmured. What fool had said that? "They do not vary, *mon ami* Tono, they do not vary. And, what is even sadder, neither do we."

Tono did not fully grasp all Voltaire's epigrammatic and allusive idiom, but he grasped that his companion had been upset, and said to comfort him: "Oh, well, we're not likely to see her again, are we?"

"And that is where you are so wrong. *Hélas*, we shall see her again. Often. Every day. The Highly Insured Legs is not of a type who will gladly bore herself alone when there are male Legs in a rich and well-furnished establishment at ten minutes' distance; her soul it shrinks in solitude as *la lingerie* shrinks in the wash."

"Then why did she come to live down here at all?"

"Because, my innocent, she is—how do you say it in your tongue?—she is down on her uppers. And the Casetta Sans Gêne, which is not a casetta at all but a piece of nonsense with a roof on it, has been lent to her without that she pays rent. Unless Monsieur Korda shall give her a rôle, and I will wager she was talking through her green collar and that he has never even heard of her existence, we will not be free of either of them for many long weeks."

Voltaire, as usual, was right. And unluckily the Relative Legs, who would have expressed herself in much the same fashion on the subject, and perhaps might have been more efficient than any male Legs in getting rid of the intruders, was away on a visit to friends in Italy. She had left Voltaire behind, as the Villa Arabesque seemed to suit him and he was getting a little old for travel: "Though, *Chien*, had I known about this, it would not have been the heat of railway-carriage floors that would have kept me here," reflected the griffon bitterly, feeling himself exposed to a more perilous furnace.

The peace of the villa was broken; the Highly Insured Legs and Dulcibel were lightly running in and out at all times and nearly every day; wanting refreshment; wanting admiration; wanting, above all, listeners to their endless egotistic film chatter:

"My Legs says we're quite *pro bono publico* up here with all of you."

As usual, Tono had to have this explained to him afterwards by Voltaire: "She means *persona grata*. But she is nearer the truth in her error than in her intention."

"Oh," said Tono. "Oh, yes, I see. Quite. Yes."

"Sweet Prince!"

However disgruntled Voltaire felt, he could always get a gleam of pleasure from his secret joke about Tono.

"Tell me, *mon petit*, have you ever been in love?"

Tono shook his head, and thumped his tail

several times because the Master Legs had just come into the room with a nondescript Visitor Legs.

"We can have a look at the map now," he said, going over to the bookcase and taking down a volume, "though I doubt if I can get away for so long until August. The voyage would take us all of six weeks."

The Visitor Legs said: "August would be hot for the Greek Islands."

"Yes, but there are the sailing races at Antibes in July, and I'm entered for three of the events. Here we are—" He had the atlas open, and the other Legs came and looked over his shoulder.

"I'd like to beat right down the Dalmatian coast, and then—"

Tono did not hear the rest. He was ruminating on the Dalmatian coast. Here was yet another item to add to the mysterious creature he was building up in his mind, from stray things heard. Dalmatian. What *is* Dalmatian? He had a cart and a coast and—what was the other thing?—a spot, or was it spots? Perhaps he'll show them to me one day. Funnily enough,

Tono never doubted but that he would eventually meet a Dalmatian and hobnob with him, ride in his cart, run down his coast, ask him to change his spots.

The Master Legs and his friend departed.

"You have not yet replied to my question?" Voltaire persisted.

Tono woke from his dream of Dalmatians: "Question? What ques— Oh, have I ever been in love? No, I don't think so. No."

"Yet you are now—how old? Three years. When I was three . . . His eyes goggled and his dry nose took on a little moisture.

"But, you see, I've been here all the time, and there was no one to fall in love with."

"Not, *par exemple*, the other dachshunds? Elsa?"

"Elsa and I were brought up together like brother and sister. I'd have made her a good husband, but I don't regret that the Legs arranged it differently. Though, mind you"— Tono was a little resentful "I can't help feeling— correct me if I'm unreasonable—I can't help feeling it was rather rude of them to overlook what is actually in the villa. Twice, now, the

Master Legs has taken her to Monte Carlo. It isn't as though I were deformed! I should say I was exceptionally sound in wind and limb. Still, there you are; they took her to Monte Carlo."

"*Il faut être philosophe. La petite* Erda? She has something more, that one, than *beauté du diable*. I find particularly seductive how the black runs into golden brown at her armpits. Are you, then, perhaps in love with Erda?"

"No, no. There was a brief period in the early spring when she seemed to me not wholly unattractive—" (Tono thoroughly disapproved of Voltaire's favourite word "seductive," and never used it himself), "but the Legs sent her away on a holiday and said something about 'next time.' Perhaps they were right. She was— she is —too young to marry. Though I'd have made her a good husband. And at the moment, though I admit her looks, she's lost her attraction for me."

"Then there is Eva. But you do not like Eva."

Tono started. Did the griffon guess everything and always guess right? It was like magic.

"No, you do not like Eva at all. Perhaps even you hate her, but that does not exclude the possibility of love. And she is provocative, that little one. Not an established beauty like Erda, but *mutine, espiègle, taquineuse, moqueuse* . . . *Enfin*, I am ready to believe, my Hamlet, that you are madly in love with Eva."

Tono shook his head: "I'm for a quiet life, and Eva's the type to go gay even after she's married. Though mind you, Voltaire, I should make her a good husband; tolerant, easy-going, yet not too easy-going, if you follow me. Eva ought to marry someone older than herself," he growled, "who would stop all this gadding about on the high seas."

"I have noticed once or twice," remarked that wicked Voltaire, "how she looks up to you."

"Yes?" Tono never suspected a double meaning in anything. "That may be, but on the whole I prefer Erda. When the time comes—"

"What time?"

"Next time"—vaguely.

"You will propose to her?"

"I've almost made up my mind. It wouldn't

be a love match, but those that aren't are often the happiest. I have the greatest respect for the Supreme Legs and shouldn't stand in the way of her worshipping him; she can still sleep at his feet if she wants to, and I'd remain next door with the Master Legs. There's plenty of time during the day."

"Time for what?"

Tono did not read Shakespeare, or he would have said: "Silken dalliance." Nor was he a coarse dog, or he would have said: "Getting down to it." He sighed, walked round within his own circle on the sitting-room floor to clear away the tall jungle grasses, flumped down and lay there motionless except for a sigh which every now and then heaved his flanks: for the Master Legs had just now spoken of a voyage, a long sea voyage to the Greek Islands, which would take all of six weeks; and Eva would go with him. Eva, always Eva!

CHAPTER NINE

VOLTAIRE HAD no illusions. Bitterly honest when in session with himself, he admitted what had happened to him. He had fallen for Dulcibel. He had no illusions about her, either. His eyes were wide open. She was without grace of birth, breeding or ancestry to recommend her; and, worst of all, she had no brains to redeem her from utter mediocrity. Her points were all wrong; her Legs was all wrong; and although nowadays no animal would be narrow-minded enough to blame another for going on the films, Voltaire was convinced that she had no talent, only a vulgar desire for celluloid publicity. No; vain, silly, bogus little mongrel lady-dog, not worthy of the name of bitch, that was Dulcibel; that was his enchantress.

He let his beard grow long, and spent many lonely hours in the dank shut-off corner he had dug out for himself, away from the villa and the other dogs. And always, writhing in self-contempt, he reached the same conclusion. He was helpless. He was humiliated. He could not free himself from thrall. Canine nature being what it is, he had known from the first whiff what he was in for. "I shall be worse before I am better," he growled:

> *"O toi, qui vois la honte ou je suis descendue,*
> *Implacable Vénus, suis-je assez confondue!*
> *Tu ne saurais plus loin pousser ta cruauté.*
> *Ton triomphe est parfait."*

How he longed to tear at her wide white ruff, worry it, draggle it . . . *la volupté*. . . . And, thus musing, he caught cold. It was a *very* dank corner of the garden, and a dog who was also a philosopher should have known better than to select it for his hermitage. The Relative Legs, returning from Florence, immediately clapped him into a warm flannel coat, bottle-green, and confined him to the villa or the hottest patch of sunshine on the terrace. Thus he was present at the first encounter between the Relative Legs and the Highly Insured Legs; an encounter conducted with freezing politeness on the one side, and a sulky annoyance, barely concealed, on the other. For the Highly Insured Legs obviously preferred a villa full of males; and suffered, moreover, from the pretty delusion that the Supreme Legs had a special tenderness for herself.

Suddenly those few sentences were spoken which were Voltaire's doom:

"You have such a dear little dog, my brother tells me. A Pomeranian. Where is he?"

"She," corrected the Highly Insured Legs. "She's down at the Casetta. I've had to shut her up."

"Tomorrow, perhaps," said Tono, trying to cheer him. It was unusual for the griffon to be in despair. Usually his mood never varied from a detached but cheerful cynicism.

"*Mais je te dis*, we shall not see her up here tomorrow, nor the day after, nor for a long, long while. And I cannot bear it; my whole system is poisoned; till the poison is out . . . *mais toi, tu ne comprends rien.*

My sufferings are formidable!"

Tono yawned, which was with him a sign of embarrassment, not of boredom. But really, for Voltaire of all dogs to break down and declare his sufferings as formidable!

"Perhaps," he suggested lamely, "if she can't come up to visit us, we shall be taken down to see her."

Voltaire's moustaches quivered in mockery. "Receive my assurance, *mon ami*, that we will not be taken down to the Casetta Sans Gêne. The Legs were not born yesterday."

"No, of course they weren't," Tono agreed, literal as usual. "But cheer up, Voltaire. We needn't ask permission, you know. What's to prevent you, if you feel like that, from slipping off to see her this evening when we're taken for our walk?"

"I will tell you what is to prevent me. *Cette sacrée jacquette de laine.*"

"What?"

"Thees damn' jacket"—briefly.

"Oh!" Tono searched in his mind for something comforting to say even about the flannel coat, but found it difficult. He hesitated between: "She might not notice it in the dark," and "Some bitches like a dressy dog," but in the end he said neither. Voltaire went on:

"It makes me ridiculous; it is badly cut; and green, it is not my colour. How can I show myself like this, in front of them all?"

"But there'll only be her."

Voltaire contradicted him with some peevishness: "Naturally there will be a crowd."

"But there are no other dogs round here for miles." Tono was astonished at Voltaire's pertinacity. The latter merely reiterated: "A crowd. There will be a crowd."

On the broader terrace below, Fafnir and Wotan were playing at Blue Train and Golden Arrow; chasing each other madly round, utter-

ing shrill yelps, till they formed an almost unbroken circle, the nose of one touching the stern
of the other.

"*Non, parbleu, non.* I cannot go down to
her; it is impossible. Everything is against me.
If I had your looks . He rolled one sick eye towards Tono, and left it there, glaring.

"Oh, come now"—modestly; "plenty of
people might say that my nose is too long and
my forelegs too short; though, mind you, I don't
agree that we dachses carry our bodies too near
the ground. Besides, a glossy coat is only skin-
deep. I've often envied you for being so witty
and cultured and knowing just what to say and
when to say it. I'm an inarticulate sort of dog,
and—What's the matter?"

The griffon had ceased to gnaw his paws;
his eyes were suddenly lucent with a strange
whimsical fire: "But it is an idea," he murmured.
"Certainly it is an idea. More, it is an inspira-
tion." And he began to chuckle softly, rocking
himself from side to side: "*Cher* Rostand, I thank
you. Never before perhaps, have I done you
justice. 'A little too much of the rant,' have I
said to myself, sitting in harsh judgment, 'too

flamboyant, *trop de panache*, this Cyrano of yours. But now: '*Je serai ton esprit, tu seras ma beauté*—'"

"I like recitations," said Tono. "I'm not good at them, but I *like* them," and he composed himself to listen to more.

"On the contrary, my friend, action!" Voltaire was in quite a different mood now, hopeful, chattering, a little feverish, and every now and then rolling over in a quite inexplicable fit of sardonic laughter.

He expected, Tono thought ruefully, when the matter had been explained, the devil of a lot.

However, he had offered to do what he could, and he was not withdrawing now. Apparently Voltaire's plan was to send him as emissary to plead his cause with Dulcibel. Some crazy notion he had that he could, as it were, use Tono's looks as though they were his own, provided Tono exactly repeated his words; his witty, cultured, allusive words; his persuasive, mischievous, delicately flattering, boldly seductive words; a complete wooing by rote. And Voltaire repeated: "'*je serai ton esprit*' (and Dog knows you need it), *'tu seras ma beauté—'*"

"Well," began Tono, "it sounds funny to me, but . . ."

When the Master Legs took them for their walk that evening, Tono had a little trouble in detaching himself and slipping away on his embassy; for the avenue and paths were washed clear by moonlight, and Elsa was in a tiresome mood and kept on asking him where he was going, each time he branched away from their routine run. It was no good taking Elsa into his confidence; her nature was essentially not in sympathy with Dulcibel's; she had once said something very sharp indeed about Dulcibel's grandmother; bitches were such women about each other.

At last, however, he thought he had successfully eluded the eye and the whistle of his beloved Master Legs. No need to go on the road either, though it was lonely enough even by day, and lonelier by night. But there was a path which ran under the pines and took one or two loops before it finally dribbled away into the scrub and burrage and wild anemones at the back of the Casetta Sans Gêne. Here at the end of the garden was a crooked goatshed, in the shadow of a clump of olives too old to bear fruit. And Voltaire had seemed to think it most likely that Dulcibel would be sleeping shut up in this shed instead of, as usual, petted and privileged on a cushion beside the bed of the Highly In-sured Legs.

"What makes you think that?" Tono had asked. "It's so unlikely."

But Voltaire, the omniscient, had merely replied: "You will find that it *is* so."

Really Voltaire was a very wonderful dog; very wonderful indeed. One could be proud to have him as a constant companion; prouder still to be chosen as his representative in courtship.

As Tono pattered down the path, he re-peated to himself conscientiously the lines Voltaire had taught him; anxious to acquit him-self with fluency and ease when he finally had to say them to Dulcibel. A pretty little thing, Dulcibel; well-meaning, too, thought Tono in amiable benediction; not much brains, but there, Voltaire had enough for seven. Besides, Voltaire, now he came to think of it, had said nothing about brains, though a great deal about passion: *"Un baiser"*—something? what was it? *"Un.point rose qu'on met sur l'i du verbe aimer. . . . Un secret qui–qui"*—so much more difficult to remember it all in French—*" Un instant d'infini qui fait un bruit d'abeille."* All about a kiss. And Voltaire, instructing him, had snapped: "But try a little to say it as if it *meant* something, *parbleu*. You are not an automate or are you? A kiss . . . *voyons*, swift, subtle, seductive" And Tono had replied: "I'm not one for kissing much, and with all due respect, Voltaire, it's not nice to get all excited the way you do, and use those words. The point is, do you want me to make her an offer of marriage on your behalf?" And Voltaire had exclaimed: *"Que je souffre!"* No more. And, on being pressed, had snuffled and sneezed and spat out in a fury: *"Mariage! Les noces! Le dot!* No, you are too, too *bourgeois. Va*, and you need say nothing about marriage."

That was the trouble with these Dulcibels (Tono wagged his head sagely)—they would tickle a dog's fancy, but they couldn't win his respect. And how very lucky, mused Tono, now quite near to the clump of olives and the shed at the back of the Casetta Sans Gêne, how *very* lucky that she has no charm for me. No charm at all. No charm—

Suddenly he stood stockstill; his heart thumping madly against his ribs.

No charm? Dulcibel? Was he mad? Tono began to tremble violently. Why, the whole wood was reeling with her charm. The moon was brilliant with her charm. . . .

"I . . . I don't feel well," murmured Tono. "Must be the heat." But he trembled as though he were as cold as poor little Voltaire, up there at the Villa Arabesque.

Voltaire. The memory was a shock. He was on his way, not to plead his own cause, but on a vicarious errand of love. Voltaire was his friend; he had to be loyal, but all the while some potent magic flowed from Dulcibel (oh, divine, oh, heavenly Dulcibel) luring him to become a traitor, to woo her for himself instead of for the griffon! He had only to turn the corner (he knew this path well) and there would be the gnarled olives crouching over the goat-shed which to-night was a palace of romance in a stream of silvery light.

"Oh, Dog," groaned poor Tono, who believed in the highest standards of friendship. "Oh, Dog, appear now and help me!"

But no vision appeared, huge and beneficent; and Tono felt he could not unaided vanquish this fatal desire for Dulcibel which was stealing over him and wrapping him round like music from the Venusberg, sapping him of honour—

Hardly knowing that he moved, he went forward, obeying the music.

. . . Immobile, menacing, as though carved out of dazzling white chalk splotched in a dazzling black pattern—*who* was it, *what* was it, standing there in the moonlight beside the goat-shed of Dulcibel's captivity? Not Great Dog himself; no, only half as big, though much, much bigger than a dachshund.

Bigger, indeed, than any mortal dog of Tono's ken.

Who was it? *What* was it?

He glared and growled at Tono. And Tono knew now. It was Anti-Dog: an incarnation risen to confront him, dappled and obscene, of his own sin, his own lust, taking concrete shape.

And Tono knew, also, without a shadow of doubt, what he had to do.

Dazed and terrified, aware that he was bound to be killed, he sprang straight for the monster's throat.

You have to vanquish sin and lust and treachery, or be for ever vanquished yourself.

It could not really be called a fight, for it was over so quickly. There was a swirl and a confusion of legs and lashing tails and snapping jaws; mingled with the high shrill barks of Dulcibel hurling herself against the door of the shed; and screams, high and shrill, from Dulcibel's mistress as she tore up the garden from the Casetta: "Oh, save him! Save him!" . . . Then Tono felt a stranglehold on his collar. He was dragged off the enemy, resisting every inch of the way, and scolded in a voice of thunder, a beloved familiar voice: the Master Legs, after all, must have seen him slip away, and had followed him down, arriving just in time.

The enemy seized his chance. For an instant there was a white streak among the glossy trunks of the olives, and then he vanished for ever.

"Why can't you keep your horrid dog shut

up?" cried the Highly Insured Legs. She had had a fright, and was in a tantrum, and had never much liked the Master Legs anyhow.

"Why can't you keep *your* little beast shut up? Properly, I mean, not in that transparent bit of lattice-work? You know perfectly well that we've got dogs up at the villa."

"If you had them under proper control—"

"Control my foot! We've been here for years, haven't we? And then you come barging in—" The Master Legs had also had a fright, and was suffering from reaction; the hand shook which grasped Tono's collar; though even now he did not pick up his little dog and carry him home under his arm, fondling him, comforting him; no, not even now, when he had so nearly lost him for ever in the huge jaws of Anti-Dog.

"You ought to give him the biggest thrashing he's ever had."

"You needn't worry. My own dog is my own business. I can give you the name of a decent vet if you don't want to be bothered with that nasty bit of work while she—"

"She's not a nasty bit of work. She's My Own Dulcibel. She gets paid £50 a week, and she's worth twenty times £50 to me."

"That's all right. I'm not arguing."

"Yes, you are. You said we were barging in. We don't want to barge, Dulcie and me. We're used to being welcome wherever we go. As welcome as the flowers in May. We're used to intellectual companionship, not savages who don't even keep their savage dogs on leads but let them spring at other dogs' throats. Tomorrow I'll pack and tomorrow we'll go and you'll be sorry."

"Good night," said the Master Legs briefly, not contesting the latter pronouncement. He looped his handkerchief through Tono's collar, and, holding both ends firmly, marched him up the hill and back to the villa. There he put him through a thorough examination, discovered that he was not hurt beyond a small bite above one eye which he sponged and dressed, but all the while without a single loving word or caress. And then, telling him in stern tones that he was in deep disgrace and ought to be ashamed of himself and would not be forgiven for a long time, he took him out to the stable instead of upstairs to the dear bedroom; and, as before when Tono had leapt into the dinghy, abandoned him to his sorrow and perplexity.

It was Voltaire, after all, who understood best what had happened, when Tono was released twenty-four hours later, and they were able at last to get some private conversation; Voltaire alone who would realise and appreciate the courageous spirit which had caused Tono to hurl himself at the throat of a dog at least thrice the size of a little dachshund. For courage, after all (reflected Voltaire), is not what we do, but what we believe we are doing.

"I admire you, *mon ami,*" said Voltaire. His cold was much better this morning; almost gone; and, though he still wore his bottle-green flannel coat, it sat on him in a less despondent fashion; one button hung loose by its thread. "Were it in my paws, you should have the *Croix de guerre* for this. But, alas, I have not the same influence any more as once in high quarters. As for that little matter which you call treachery to me—bah! I mock myself of that. *C'est une bagatelle.* Montaigne says truly, 'We seek and offer ourselves to be gulled.'"

"I wouldn't have betrayed you, you know,

if it had actually come to it," Tono faltered. "At least, I think I wouldn't. I feel sure I wouldn't. My better self . . . one is tempted . . . but if it had actually come to it . . . "

"But naturally you would not!" And to himself: "But naturally you would." For Voltaire saw no reason, out of this mass of motive and countermotive, self-delusion and sentimentality, to revise his opinion: *"Plus je vois les chiens, plus j'aime les hommes."* Still, if it made it a little easier and happier for that poor forlorn Tono, that comical victim of Looking-Glass-Land, to squat there solemnly unwinding yards of mystic macaroni about Dog and Anti-Dog and incarnations, spells and charms and visions and the romantic lure of beauty in the moonlight, let him meander on.

"—I must have fallen in love with her subconsciously that very first time the Highly Insured Legs brought her up here."

"They're leaving," the griffon announced carelessly.

"What? Who? Leaving where?"

"Leaving the Casetta Sans Gêne."

"Both of them?"

"*Mais oui*, both. They do not like it any more. It is too *triste* a neighbourhood. And they have not been given an *accueil* warm enough, up here at the Arabesque. My Legs, now she has returned, was a little outspoken in her opinion of the Highly Insured Legs; and the Master Legs, on the night of your adventure, spoke a little brutally—"

Tono nodded: "I was there."

"Yes, you were there. And, *enfin*, the Highly Insured Legs lost her temper and did not recover it; and hoped for a message from the Supreme Legs, an invitation to dine, shall we say? Only it did not come, that invitation. She thought, *vois-tu*, that she was a *Spécialité de la Maison*, but, on the contrary, 'e 'ate 'er guts." Voltaire at moments was very low in his talk. "And so they pack their trunks and they depart today —tomorrow—at once. It has been a failure."

"But, Voltaire, how do you know all this?" Tono had never been further from understanding life and its complexities and manifestations and injustices. He could not forget how the Master Legs had scolded his little Tono (not very hard) and exclaimed: "You might have killed him!" And now here was Voltaire, with a more righteous claim to censure him, so serene in his mood, so loftily raised above the claims of the flesh and the fevers of love. Not even minding that Dulcibel was going away.

"How did you know?" Tono repeated.

"Dulcibel told me."

"You've seen her?" shouted Tono.

"What is the matter that you shout? Yes, indeed, I have seen her, the foolish little one. She ran up to leave her card on me, *pour prendre congé*. It was easy to slip off, with her Legs so busy in preparation for departure; she told me she came in person, though it was unconventional, because she felt the need, after so much indelicacy and upset, for a little intellectual conversation."

"Well?" said Tono. And by "Well?" he meant: And did you have an opportunity of telling her how much you loved her? how you worshipped the ground her little paws spurned so lightly? Did you, in fact, pour forth all that burden of longing, of timid and reverential desire with which you charged me not two days ago?

"*Well?*"

"There was no intellectual conversation." And Voltaire delicately removed from his flannel coat a clinging white cotton hair. He liked to be neat.

CHAPTER TEN

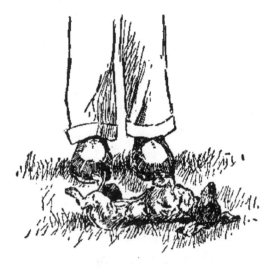

June came in that summer in a bright blaze. And immediately Tono moved into the shade, and was limp and unenthusiastic and sighed a lot. The other dogs did not seem to mind the sun so much; and the twins especially grew in length and activity every day.

Erda objected to the hot weather, because it meant that she was ejected from the bed of the Supreme Legs, and made to sleep on the parquet instead. One night she woke from a beautiful dream in which she, while remaining Erda, was somehow also his knitted pullover and he wore her all the time. . . . For a moment on waking she was bitterly disappointed; then realised that a glad thing had happened during her sleep: a cold snap had come. A leap and a scramble and she was in Paradise again, snuggling down, snuggling close; *lovely* cold weather, ice, snow and a north wind. So now everything could be as it was before, and all was light and happiness.

The next morning, the heat wave was a matter beyond doubt, and the Supreme Legs came down to breakfast with dark circles under his eyes, and complained of having slept badly:

"Erda seemed to be under a misapprehension that it was winter at last. During most of the night I couldn't tell which was her and which was my feet; they were all three equally hot, and I couldn't get rid of any of them."

"Wish-fulfilment," explained the Master Legs.

"Hers. Not mine."

"Tono seems quite overcome. Hi, old boy, don't you like the weather?"

Tono thumped his tail, feebly opened one eye and closed it again. He said to himself: A quiet day, I think; no chasing round; leave that to the puppies. Towards evening, perhaps, when it gets cooler, Voltaire and I might take a stroll through the long grass; nothing energetic.

The Relative Legs was reading the local paper. Now she remarked: "There's a special Dachshund Show at Nice on the 17TH. Princesse de Chauvenet is awarding the prizes. She has eleven dachshunds of her own."

"*That* old woman! She's had four husbands, too, and couldn't get one of them to stay with her for more than twenty minutes."

This seemed to Tono, remembering Elsa's conjugal sagas and anecdotes, a good average length for a husband's stay with a wife; and he wondered sleepily why the Master Legs used that jeering tone.

The Relative Legs went on chattily: "It's a pity your dogs are so badly trained, or we might enter them."

"Badly trained?" shouted the Master Legs.

The Supreme Legs laid down *The Times* and gazed at his sister with mournful speculative eyes. If only his parents had had all sons, if only he had nothing but brothers, if only she had been a younger sister so that he could have sat on her head more frequently throughout their childhood

"Badly trained?" repeated the Master Legs. "Our dogs *badly* trained?"

"My mistake. I should have said not trained at all. Why, good heavens, the puppies haven't even learnt how to follow you. Elsa doesn't come when you call her, and makes life one long mealtime. And, though she's supposed to be clever, she can't do a single trick. None of them can. I gave Tono a small parcel to carry the other day, just up the avenue, and he dropped it fifty-two times and licked it and chewed it and worried it, till afterwards it was no use to me at all."

"What was it?"

"A hair-net."

"We don't train our dogs to carry hair-nets"—with dignity.

"You don't train them at all; that's what I'm complaining of. Not that it has anything to do with me. But I think it's a pity. Erda's quite nice-looking; she's got all the right points, but—"

"Right. We'll enter Erda for the Nice show. I'll write in today."

"She's hopelessly timid with strangers. Directly she sees the judges, she'll give an imitation of a black pancake squirming. And that won't get her any prizes."

"We'll see about that," the Master Legs declared briskly. And a faint sensation of uneasiness ran through the dogs grouped under and around the breakfast-table. Why couldn't the Relative Legs hold her silly tongue? What was going to happen to them? What new and agitating element might be introduced into their peaceful lives, today of all days when the weather had begun to be hot and languorous?

Their worst forebodings were presently realised. Stung by her taunts, the Master Legs spent the whole morning firmly though not unkindly training the Arabesque dogs. He did not seem to notice the weather; nor was he easily discouraged. From cool and comfortable vantage on an upper terrace, Voltaire looked on and was amused. Nobody tried to train *him*.

Life was dreadfully unfair. They had a dreadful time.

The Master Legs began with Erda. It was a serious business, preparing Erda for the show on the 17TH. On the advice of the Relative Legs, who, now that she had had her say, was in a more amiable mood, frequent rehearsals were the best way of accustoming her to the sight of strangers. So he roped in the entire household, plus the wife, sister and two babies of the second gardener, to come and sit in a ring on the terrace, and to behave as much as possible in the manner of an inconsiderate and fidgety audience.

"The judges have to be strangers," insisted the Relative Legs, "or the test is no good at all. And they must know how a judge is likely to handle and examine Erda."

So the Master Legs rang up some friends who had a house-party, and asked them (to their surprise) not to come themselves but to send any male members of their party who had never been at the Villa Arabesque before, but knew tolerably well how to handle a nervous dog. This arranged, he left his improvised audience sitting in a ring on the terrace, with no objection to this odd fashion of being kept from their normal morning jobs; and filled up the time till the judges should arrive by an attempt to train Tono to "fetch on command." First he rolled a pair of gloves into a ball, and called Tono to attend. He then threw the gloves to the far end of the terrace. Tono tore after them and picked them up.

"There you are!" said the Master Legs in triumph to a sceptical Relative Legs.

Tono began to worry the gloves.

"No. Fetch them here. Fetch. Fetch. Good dog, Tono! Oi! Come on! *Fetch!*"

Tono dropped the gloves where they lay, and trotted back to the Master Legs, gazed dumbly and lovingly up in his face, wagged his tail, and oozed from every pore the desire to die for his master.

"That's no good," said the Relative Legs. "And he mustn't bring it back and drop it, either. He must learn to give it gently into your hands."

The process was repeated six–seven–eight–nine times.

"Of course, one has to have a little patience," said the Relative Legs.

The tenth time, Tono brought back the gloves in his mouth; but, entering warmly into the spirit of the game, refused either to drop them or to deliver them, as commanded, into his master's hand. He planted himself in front of the Master Legs, the gloves firmly gripped between his teeth, and dared him to take them away. When the Master Legs pulled at a portion, Tono held on even more firmly to the rest, and began to dance, to throw himself backwards, to let his paws slide forward, to turn the training into a merry tug-of-war.

"Drop!" said the Master Legs in a voice of thunder.

Tono pulled the gloves away, bounded through the archway at the far end of the terrace into the wild part of the garden, and dropped them into the pool of goldfish, hoping that the Master Legs would be satisfied and say "Good dog, Tono," and allow him to go away happy.

The Master Legs was getting a little impatient. He did not like the bright remarks from the Relative Legs, nor the expression of

Voltaire's moustaches from the upper terrace, nor the shouts of merry Gallic laughter and applause from the staff, still sitting in a circle on the terrace. Luckily at this moment the friends of his friends drove up in a fast car, and took their places with due solemnity as judges at the dog show. Tono was released and Erda's trial began.

"Why don't they learn to carry their own parcels?" remarked Elsa in a sarcastic aside to Tono. "You were quite right to make a stand. I would never dream of allowing either Eva or Erda to do anything of the sort."

"Erda seems a little miserable about something," said Tono, watching her not unkindly. He had never had reason to be jealous of Erda as of Eva.

Poor Erda, though no one could doubt her beauty and breeding, was a hopeless failure in show deportment. All attempts to make her trot into the ring with a bold defiant carriage of the head and an alert intelligent expression, merely resulted in her lying flat and abject, with pathetic little whimpers whenever either of the two unknowns picked her up or even touched her. Reproved with some sternness by the Master Legs, she rolled over on her back, waggled her paws piteously, and moaned like a dying dachs in a thunderstorm. Then the Supreme Legs picked her up and pretended to examine her. Ecstasy from Erda; eyes sparkling, nose quivering, tail thumping: "Do with me what you will, beloved!"

That was all very well, but it was most unlikely, they all agreed, that the Supreme Legs would be elected as one of the judges; he was no expert. The rehearsal judges tried once more. They said that Erda was so perfect, it was a pity she could not learn enough poise and confidence to make it worth while entering her for the competition.

Immediately Erda lay flat again, trembled and died several times.

The Relative Legs laughed.

"Oh, well," declared the Master Legs, discouraged but still determined, "as Eva isn't six months old yet, it'll have to be Elsa. She'll need the devil of a lot of grooming and brushing for the next ten days. I'll give her a bath presently, to begin with."

"Thank you," said Elsa, and shot away into the kitchen. The ring was broken, the staff dismissed to their duties, the friends of the friends thanked and given drinks.

"Jolly little chaps," they said, indicating the puppies.

The Relative Legs said: "It's a pity they haven't been taught to follow yet, so one can't take them for walks, and their dew-claws are getting much too long. They'd soon wear them out along the roads if only they could learn how to follow. You see," she continued, making quite sure that the friends of the friends did see, "they don't follow. They haven't been trained."

The Master Legs, grinding his teeth, took Fafnir and Wotan and gave them a lesson in keeping to heel. The first essential was the fixing of a collar and a long lead attached. Fafnir and Wotan had never yet worn collars. Their bodies became surprisingly flexible in resistance. The Master Legs was nearly exhausted by the time he had achieved his object, but they were as fresh as ever.

"It requires patience, of course," said the Relative Legs.

The Master Legs explained his method to everyone beforehand, so that there should be no doubt about it.

Taking first one puppy and then the other, the plan was to trot them along the terrace at the end of the lead, and then invite them to follow with the lead long and slack. If they were obdurate and sat down, rooted themselves in the ground and tried to pull in the reverse direction, a gentle tug was to be given to the lead and at the same time the command "Heel" should ring out on the balmy air. "That's *your* side of it," said the Relative Legs. "Now we'll see theirs."

". . . *Mais c'est formidable*," murmured Voltaire half an hour later, from the terrace above.

"Afraid we'll have to push off," said the friends of the friends.

"You ought to have begun it at least a month ago," said the Relative Legs.

Gleaming with sweat, the Master Legs lifted his voice and commanded that Elsa, a bath-tub and the disinfectant should be placed on the patch of sunlight outside the kitchen door.

Elsa, her whereabouts under the kitchen sink betrayed by the Butler Legs, was carried struggling to her doom. Erda and Eva and the puppies sat round in a solemn group and watched their mother go through ignominy and sorrow. All Elsa's cool materialism, her philosophic acceptance of life, departed when it was brought in contact with soap and water. The presence of her offspring, bone-dry and deeply interested, made the ordeal a hundred times worse.

"I'll never have another litter as long as I live, so help me Dog," she growled between her teeth. Not often was she low and coarse enough to call her family "litter."

She tried to bite the Relative Legs who was holding her. She tried to bite the Master Legs who was soaping her. She perfectly understood (and it did not help) that she was only undergoing this torture as a mere second choice to Erda for the show.

Tono lay with his back to everybody, flumped down and brooding on the now deserted terrace: no question, if you please, of entering *him* for the Dachshund Show. Oh, no.

Oh, dear me, no. The name of Tono had not even been brought up for consideration. Erda had proved a failure, and Eva and the puppies were under six months old, and Elsa had been chosen. But did anyone suggest Tono? One Legs among the lot? No, he was too clumsy, too ugly, too underbred for prizes and shows. All they could do to *him* was to tire him out by throwing a silly old pair of gloves rolled into a ball and shouting "Fetch!" on the hottest morning of the summer.

He did not stir, even when Elsa, rolled in a rough towel, was carried past the flickering shade under the eucalyptus tree where he lay sulking, and laid tenderly in the gilded sunlight to get dry and recover breath and temper. She was followed by the little troupe of her progeny; and they were presently joined by the griffon, who in a series of terse well-chosen prose vignettes described to each of them how they had seemed from the viewpoint of an onlooker above, during their various trials of the morning.

The Master Legs, hot and weary, picked up Eva, and announced that he was going off on the yacht for the rest of the day: the water was fit for bathing at last, and he surmised that a plunge in the Mediterranean might help him to forget that he had ever been fool enough to bother about dogs.

" Except Eva," he added. Which was most damnably unfair, because Eva was the only one whom he had not badgered that morning, or no doubt she would have been as obstreperous and unreachable as the rest.

But, once they had gone, the atmosphere settled into amber peace. Even Tono, wounded though he had been, could not but feel the relief from strain, and the beauty of the lazy Southern day. Even Elsa became less bitter, ate double her usual lunch, and consented to forgive her enemies. Blue butterflies wavered on the air or poised motionless on the brilliant petals of the flowering creepers which streamed down the white façade of the villa and tumbled from the terraced walls. Towards evening the day hardly seemed to wane, only thickened to a drowsier hush and deeper content. The cooing doves slid from the crest of the eucalyptus trees to the tips of the darker pines. The puppies lay sleeping blissfully on the broken nasturtiums. The Supreme Legs sat alone on the terrace and smoked his pipe and caressed Erda, supine on his knees.

Voltaire invited Tono to take a stroll into the wild part, where the long grasses grew under the olives, the foliage softly glittering in the level light, from silver to black, and black to silver. He had been, ever since lunch, in one of his rare moods when he was so winning that Tono, asking for no more excellent companion on a fine summer's evening, was able to think with an approach to equanimity of Eva and the Master Legs swinging off together to the yacht. Except for that curious little twinge of desire-to-be-carried which bit at him whenever he saw one of the other dachs in that enviable position, he now found himself reflecting that the anguish of jealousy was not nearly so tight around his heart as when Eva first went seafaring with the Master Legs. Perhaps in time it might loosen altogether and fall away, if nothing specially painful should occur. And what could occur? Nothing, because there *was* nothing. Thus Tono, without even touching wood.

On these late afternoon saunters, it was usually Voltaire who talked, Tono who listened, fascinated by the extent and depths of his companion's wisdom. From that question of unflagging interest, the muzzling order, Voltaire passed at a step to the name of Pasteur: "One of the few Very Great Legs that have ever lived," he affirmed. But Tono, drooping his head with shame had to confess that he had only once heard the name of Pasteur and had asked Elsa about it, and Elsa had shut him up quite snappishly: it was not a name she cared to hear in the mouth of any decent dog, said Elsa.

Voltaire merely shrugged: "She would naturally take the conventional attitude. With all her intelligence and experiences, Elsa is *au fond* conventional!"

Followed a brief biographical sketch of that Very Great Legs, Pasteur.

Tono was astonished, and tried not to be shocked: for Elsa was right: it was not done in the best kennels to mention or even admit that dogs ever went mad and bit Legs. Occasionally a very rude little tradesman's dog might write up the word "hydrophobia" with a snigger on the wall, but it was quickly rubbed out again and nice puppies were taught to look the other way.

Voltaire noticed Tono's jaw drop, and was amused: a freethinker, he was used to these re-actions, and had learnt during his ten long years of life not to be impatient:

"*Tenez, mon ami*, one day you will learn to look facts in the face. But for this mellow evening which, though it is June, reminds me romantically of de Musset's 'Nuit de Mai,' let us put away *les politiques* and so remain friends. You and I, at all events, will not refuse to drink water just yet."

Tono agreed that it was thirsty weather; so they hastened their steps a little, knowing that along the lower terrace and up the two short flights of garden steps, and round to the right just before you came to the statue of St. Florian, would bring them to that cool and shady bit of grass outside the kitchen door where water was always standing fresh and clear in their bowls.

"Listen," said Tono, pricking his ears, "isn't that the voice of the Master Legs?"

And he bounded forward at a quicker pace, delighted that his Legs should be home sooner than expected.

Then he stopped.

"*Eva*—" That was the name repeated over and over again in the hurly-burly of excited talk and laughter on the terrace. And Eva was being exhibited, held high in the Master Legs' arms, while he related what was apparently some dramatic story of her prowess. . . . "Eva . . . Eva. . . ." Tono drew nearer and listened, his heart thudding painfully. And at that moment some Visitor Legs arrived, so that the Master Legs had to repeat the story from the very beginning.

He told it solemnly, with considerable dramatic power: Eva had saved his life. And, though his listeners laughed, that was no doubt their hysterical reaction at hearing how he had been so near to death that, but for Eva's gallantry, he would now be lying, food for fishes, on the cold floor of the sea.

Eva, having seen him at one moment with arms raised above his head, safely standing on the boards of the yacht, and the next fallen crash into the very middle of the Mediterranean, little Eva, without a moment's hesitation, with a piercing yelp, had plunged in after him and brought him back to safety. Brave little Eva . . . splendid little Eva . . . heroic little Eva . . . her exploit lifted her on to a pinnacle of notice and adulation. Praises were showered: what presence of mind! what devotion! and she so small and the sea so large. Amidst this clamour of praise, the frequent laughter might have struck Tono as callous, had he not been too horrified and stricken to notice anything. Eva was carried off at last by the Master Legs, to be given a particularly succulent dinner. And Tono walked slowly in the opposite direction, away from the villa into the jungle, distant from everybody, and lay down, and put his nose between his paws, and wrestled blindly with despair. For this was his darkest hour.

Eva had saved the life of the Master Legs. Not he, Tono, who had always longed for the chance, but Eva. So that from now onwards, Eva, besides being the constant companion away at sea (and that had been hard enough for Tono to bear), would also be the most dearly loved at home, for ever privileged and caressed, nearest to the heart of the Master Legs.

Tono whimpered a little, racked with jealousy. Presently, however, he grew calmer, but his anguish was no less bitter. For it occurred to him that he ought not to be hating Eva but be grateful to her. How was it he could not be grateful, since she had rescued the Master Legs from drowning, and he, Tono, loved the Master Legs? This simple estimate of what his feelings should be, compared with what they were, filled Tono with disgust at himself. No other dachshund, he was convinced, would be so paltry, so egotistical, so envious as he.

Yet it was luck alone which gave Eva her glorious opportunity. When Tono had hurled himself at the throat of Anti-Dog, standing there so huge and still and menacing in the moonlight, he had risked his little life then, every bit as much, though in an abstract cause. And what had been his portion at the time? Had he been lifted tenderly and carried home in the arms of the Master Legs, and heard warm praise of his valour rising and echoing on all sides? No. Blows and harsh words; home on the lead, and then shut up in the stable in disgrace. It was not fair. Life was not fair. He could not endure it. He would end it, now, at once, before he had to see Eva and the Master Legs with this new tender filament joining them together.

Tono leapt to his feet. Dusk was falling; he need not be seen if he went up to the swimming pool, not by the long flight of steps beside the villa, but from above, by the way which once—ah, how long ago it seemed!—he had shown Voltaire on his arrival with the Relative Legs. From the land of echoes floated a whisper: "What's this I hear about your having bought a yacht?"

Alas, what indeed? That yacht had been the beginning of sorrow for him, thought Tono.

Suddenly he stopped on his fateful errand. He would drown himself, but not in the swimming pool. There he had once seen Dog. At least let him not desecrate the waters where the Vision had appeared.

So he turned, half-way up, and pattered along the path which struck off at right angles into the grove of olives. The little mossy pool where the goldfish swam would serve his purpose just as well. The goldfish would mind as little as the stars, sobbed Tono. A hope still lay couchant under his despair that Great Dog might again appear, and perhaps this time give tongue, however softly: "Tono . . .poor Tono. . . .

But no such comfort appeared in the moonless night, under the olive trees; no Vision glimmered among the darting shadows of fish.

"Good-bye, my Master Legs," whispered Tono, on the edge of the mossy pool. Then he shut his eyes tight and leapt in.

. . . But he was not drowned. He was still alive. Somehow, something, someone, was preventing him from drowning himself, however hard he tried. He sought desperately to fulfil his purpose, but the water, enchanted as the Red Sea which would not drown the Tribe of Moses, refused to rise above his knees. Somehow, something, someone, caused an invisible impediment. Someone who wished Tono to go on living. Could it be Dog?

CHAPTER ELEVEN

FOR THE NEXT few days, Tono moved about the villa and garden with Melancholy and Gentleness for his two companions. His behaviour to Eva, especially, might have brought tears to any eyes. Eva herself was puzzled by it, and rather wished he would stop. For hitherto she had always enjoyed Tono's heavy disapproval of almost everything she did or said, using it as a springboard for cheeky repartee. But now all this was changed: "Little Eva," he would murmur ("Looking at me so stupidly, Erda, like somebody tolling a bell"), and then he would turn his head away very slowly, and sigh, and droop his tail, and flump on to the parquet, and sigh again, and fix his mournful eyes anew on Eva till she ran yapping out of the room.

"Have you noticed," said the Relative Legs to the Master Legs, one morning shortly after all this turmoil of rescue and heroism, "have you noticed that Tono seems a little depressed?"

"*Noticed* it? When I take him for a walk, I come back so miserable myself that I nearly cut my throat. It's catching."

Tono, half asleep, wondered listlessly whether it would be more delicate for him to get up and move away, as he was the subject of conversation. But he had not the energy, so he merely raised his head and howled to let them know he was in the room. Manners could not demand more than that. While he was howling, he missed a phrase which made the rest of the talk too obscure for him to follow.

". . . tomorrow morning early, then," said the Master Legs.

"You'll be back before evening, and bring her along in the car, I suppose. Better let Aristide drive, so that you can devote yourself to the lady. If you go by the Moyenne Corniche, it ought to take about three hours to Beaupré."

Tono lost interest. He had never had much, but now they were not talking about him any more.

". . . She won't be brindled, you know. Johnson hasn't got any brindles."

"Does that matter?"

"No, we're not breeding champions. Our object is to bring back the sparkle to his eyes and the roses to his cheeks."

"Well, we know what he needs. And it's high time. After all, he's two years old."

"As long as you avoid a harlequin. Harlequins usually have butterfly noses like a horrid Dalmatian."

Tono pricked to attention in a moment.

"My God," said the Master Legs, "I thought there was going to be murder done the other night when Tono flew at that Dalmatian's throat

So *that* was a Dalmatian! So a Dalmatian was *that!*

Tono settled himself with this startling piece of information, and examined it from every facet. *If* that was a Dalmatian, then it was not, as he had supposed, Sin and Lust and Anti-Dog. It was just a Dalmatian. But how was he to recognise it without a dog-cart and without a coast? As for butterfly noses, honestly, when the encounter took place, he had had no time to check up on noses. Black spots? Yes, he remembered in what a sinister pattern they had stood out against the dazzling white of the big dog's coat. All his life he had wanted to hob-nob with a Dalmatian, and then, when they did meet, they had fought.

Now isn't that life all over? reflected Tono, mourning for lost glamour. And the Master Legs had said: "I thought there would be murder done." Well, why, if he had felt his little Tono had been in danger of murder, had he been so cross? Why harsh words and severe chastisement? Why not have treated him rather as one restored by a miracle from the slavering jaws of death?

Tono blew a heavy sigh. The waters were muddy which should have been limpid. However, by listening, the Dalmatian mystery had been illuminated for ever. Perhaps by listening further . . .

But the conversation at the table above him had drifted back to the same boring subject as before: harlequins and so forth; a subject of no importance to Tono. He yawned and sighed again and yawned again.

"I think harlequins are amusing, but Johnson hasn't got any of those, either. His are all fawn or blue."

"Blue, then," said the Relative Legs.

"Fawn," decreed the Supreme Legs. "Fawn will mate better with brindle."

The Master Legs had been away all day. This time he did not take Eva with him, even though she had saved his life.

The hours passed in drowsy procession, and Eva complained that nothing ever happened at the Arabesque. Elsa told them a fairy story, but the puppies wandered away in the middle, and she complained that she did not know what she had done to deserve such an ungrateful family. Erda suddenly got the illusion that the Supreme Legs was going away and would never return. She had no grounds for believing this; unless perhaps Eva in a mischievous mood had suggested it to tease her; so she did not let him for one moment out of her sight, and her attentions when he tried to have a bath became definitely embarrassing.

The Relative Legs had clipped Voltaire's coat in a desultory amateurish way, because of the heat and ticks. Voltaire was furious, though Tono and Elsa hastened to assure him it was a great improvement:

"*Zut alors*, that is what all the friends of Samson they say to him after Delilah 'as shorn 'im uneven! 'You 'ave no idea, Samson old man, 'ow much better!' . . . *je m'en fiche de vos compliments.*"

"Just as you say, Voltaire. I'm sure you're right."

Voltaire, bored by so much other-cheek, tried to stimulate Tono into a quarrel. But for Tono, Voltaire's salt had lost its savour; and the griffon, in no mood to bear this wistful trickle of good and unselfish thoughts, finally shrugged his shoulders and left him. Even catching fleas was more amusing than Tono, lately.

So it happened that towards sunset Tono was alone, lying curled up at the end of the long terrace where a green archway led into the olive grove beyond, when he heard the voice of the Master Legs. And the Master Legs was calling, not Eva, but Tono.

Tono sprang alert—then checked himself. What was the good? He would only be discouraged again. He must learn to live his life without love.

But then a current of wild excitement ran down the shining air . . . and another . . . and another. Tono stiffened; ears, eyes and nostrils responding as though they were one sense instead of three. And still he could not, dared not, move. He was turned to stone. What was happening? *Who was this?*

Through the open double doors from the sitting room, standing for a moment on the top of the flight of marble steps leading down to the terrace, then advancing steadily towards him like glorious destiny—

Dog himself?

No.

Yes.

No. Smaller than Great Dog, and with certain delicate differences. A wonderful creature; a daughter of the dogs, divinely tall and most divinely fair; a vision of flexible ivory and shining cream, the sun streaming down on her satiny coat that rippled as she walked, and danced a little in her walk, tugging at her leash. And a voice like the voice of Dog himself seemed to rush from Tono's heart into Tono's mouth, saying: "This is your reward!"

(*"Tiens!"* exclaimed Voltaire, who, as usual, was watching all that went on, from a comfortable coign above, on the terrace just below the cactuses: *"Mais c'est rigolo, ça. Et maintenant? Nous verrons!"*)

The Master Legs bent down and unhooked the Vision from her leash. Then he gave Tono an encouraging pat: "Here you are, old boy," he said cheerfully.

And, after that, it was as though he had melted from the scene; he may have been there; he may have gone away. All Tono could realise, with dazzled eyes and a pulse beating madly in his nose, was that he had fallen in love, wildly, passionately in love, for the first and only time in his life.

Yet how could he, unworthy little dachshund, aspire to such nonpareil? Tono hardly dared trust himself to speak. At last, in a low hoarse voice, he suggested that she might care to take a look round, and could he have the pleasure of escorting her?

"It's rather hot out here, and perhaps you've had a long journey," he faltered. "Shall we go indoors?"

He walked along sedately, trying with all his might to keep his feelings under control— (What the hell's the matter with him? wondered the Master Legs)—but she, unfeignedly eager to make friends, pranced and galloped, was now in front of him and now behind, and now encircling him in joyful caracoles of seductive graceful wooing. Ah, but she was mocking him, as far above him as Sirius the Dog-star.

"And this is your first visit to the Riviera?" (Manners, Tono, manners! You are, after all, her host. Don't betray your passion. Never betray it.) "Are you making a long stay? Do you find the air—do you find the air—salubrious?"

It seemed she could not be bothered with trivial conversation, but she just carelessly gave him to understand that she had been born some-where down here, though a long way off, and that she believed she was staying for ever.

"We'll go round by the terrace of the orange trees. We have a very fine view of the sea from there. Do you care for yachting? I don't," Tono added quickly. "Not a bit, I don't."

Yachting meant nothing, apparently, to the Vision.

"*Good!*" said Tono in heartfelt relief.

He showed her the front hall and the famous marble staircase. Then they went into the sitting room, which was empty, and made a tour of inspection there. And all the time her restlessness grew: she bounded among the furniture; she ran at Tono and then leapt backwards; gaily she tantalised him, and then tried to console him for the torment. Tono felt he could not hold out much longer. He wondered if he should call Voltaire to assist him, and then decided he did not want Voltaire, damn him, with his witty tongue and false cynicisms.

The door into the inner courtyard was usually kept closed, but now it was open, and she rushed through it without waiting to be bidden. He followed her. She galloped round and round the courtyard, flashing in and out of the cloister pillars.

Tono had forgotten, in this crazy tumult of happiness and misery, that there was a hole in the wall, and that here he had once seen Dog. . . . Until here he saw Dog again.

Standing firmly planted opposite him, just beyond the frame, a full three feet high, his glossy coat brindled in stripes of tawny orange and black, his eyes under their heavy brows yellow and benign. . . . And then, moving up behind Great Dog, came the smaller, lovelier Vision whom Tono had left behind him, playing among the slender white pillars.

He looked back over his shoulder.

And she was here, too, moving just behind him, throwing back her graceful head, lashing her tail.

How had she crossed with such lightning quickness from one side of the frame to the other? From Dog to him?

Again Tono looked at Dog. And still she was there. Again he looked back over his shoulder. And still she was here, on this side of the frame, just behind him.

And now, tired of waiting, with an enchanting gesture she placed her forepaws on his shoulders and stood upright, facing him.

Troubled beyond all measure, he glanced sideways. The same gesture was repeated just beyond the frame. He could see it there, happening to Great Dog; but the thrilling pressure on his shoulders was here, on this side of the frame, happening to *him*.

So she was there, too, as well as here?

And Dog was here, too, as well as there?

She kissed him.

And then he knew this was reality, and that beyond the frame was only her image. He saw it happen in the mirror, but oh, he could *feel* it happen to himself—swift and subtle and seductive, the lick of her exquisite tongue. . . .

He was not a dachshund. He, Tono, was Great Dog.

CHAPTER TWELVE

CREDULITY reeled: his brain reeled; the
world reeled and swung on its pivot—

And as Tono leapt upon his mate, and she
sprang away from him and bounded through
the rooms and out into the garden, he after her,
his whole realm crashed into a song of size and
proportion. Ever since he could remember, it
had been tilted a degree awry, but now he knew
what was large and what was small; now he knew

that he was ten times bigger than any dachshund, as the pool is larger than the puddle and
the sea than the pool; now he could measure
the stately silver of the eucalyptus against the
smaller brilliance of the orange tree; the villa
furniture dwindled and shrank; everything was
right in its own place and being and dimension,
and he was blessed above all dogs.

And now, no longer cramped within the
shape of an illusion, he could release the full
strength of his limbs and the full power of his
voice; he could leap and gallop and hear the
rhythmic beat of his own thundering tread, and
rejoice in it, chasing his mate up and down the
terraces, through the jungle and the wild
part. . . .

And look with tolerance and affection upon
the little dachshunds in their lowliness, and see
that they were comical and enchanting, courageous and loyal and sweet. But now he might
cease fretting that the Legs would never call
him sweet, for he understood that the petting
and caresses for which he had so passionately
yearned were for the little dogs with their
crooked legs and trustful eyes, not for him,

never for him. But he could do without, for he
had entered into his own kingdom, able to ad-
just his life to his stature, so that there would
be no more disharmony. As he moved hence-
forth through the villa and the garden, he could
proudly claim to occupy so and so much ten-
ancy of the air, while, hardly displacing a mouth-
ful, the little dachshunds waddled and pattered
along the long terraces and spacious rooms
which were so perfect a setting for his own noble
proportions. Never again need he halt and painfully squeeze under, where now with such ease
he could leap over, and spurn as he leapt. Tono
stood still and threw back his head, and from
his massive throat he bayed and bayed
again. . . . Then once more sprang to his swaggering pursuit. They rushed past the shallow
pool where the little goldfish swam; and he remembered how he, a Goliath among dogs, had
stood knee-high in the water of that pool, and
actually tried thus to drown himself; and how,
moreover, he had leapt into the dinghy, believing he was no bigger than Eva, and had nearly
sunk the dinghy; and how he had all but killed
that poor little Dalmatian when, a prey to reli-

gious zeal, he had seized him by the throat.

And, finally, Tono saw now that what he had believed in his agony to be literal truth, had been related as a joke; yes, and a not unfunny joke. For how could intrepid little Eva, who was so tiny, have saved the life of the Master Legs, who was so tall? Tono gave her generous credit for her gallantry; ridiculous little Eva, throwing herself into the sea. Yet love had transcended her limitations, and, joke or no joke, she remained a heroine. But he, Tono, had no limitations, for he was aware not only that Dog was himself, but that he was Dog.

And, with this last exultant revelation, desire lent him even greater swiftness, and he drew alongside his bride, who had tumbled exhausted into the cool long grass under the olive trees:

"She's smaller than me, and I'm not going to stand any more nonsense."

CHAPTER THIRTEEN

THE LEGS WERE assembled in the sitting-room, with Voltaire and Erda, when they saw Tono advance towards them; proud and stately, through the archway and down the long terrace. The beautiful stranger who had been brought to the villa that afternoon walked respectfully a few paces behind him. And, indeed, there was a tranquil dignity in Tono's gait and the poise of his head which commanded esteem and justified his arrogance.

"*The beautiful stranger . . . walked respectfully a few paces behind him.*"

One of the double doors into the sitting-room always stood open during the day; but when he reached the top of the flight of steps he stood still, just beyond the threshold, and waited; not displeased at their tardiness, but kindly ready to believe that presently they would realise what was required of them.

"Why doesn't he come in?" wondered the Relative Legs. "Hi, Tono! Good dog!"

But still Tono waited with the divine patience of the very large; slowly lashing his tail for the sensuous pleasure it gave him to feel it swing in such wide and grandiose arcs. . . .

"I think," said the Supreme Legs, "I *think* that what he wants is to have the other door opened for him as well."

"Well, I'm damned," laughed the Master Legs. And went to do it.

With a slight but gracious inclination of the head—for Tono, though Dog, could appreciate and return the lesser courtesies—he passed through into the room; walking meticulously in the centre of the way, so as to be sure not to brush the jamb with his flanks; and thereby leaving enough space for at least four other Great

Danes to have walked through on either side of him.

And Voltaire, watching, sighed: the spectacle was over. He might encounter in the future many dachshunds who thought they were Great Danes; but never again, he was convinced, a Great Dane who thought he was a dachshund.